Baltimore Chronicles Volume 3

Baltimore
Chronicles
Volume 3

Treasure Hernandez

www.urbanbooks.net

Urban Books, LLC
78 East Industry Court
Deer Park, NY 11729

Baltimore Chronicles Volume 3 Copyright © 2011
Urban Books, LLC Treasure Hernandez

ISBN 13: 978-1-60162-455-0
ISBN 10: 1-60162-455-7

First Printing July 2011
Printed in the United States of America

10 9 8 7 6 5 4 3 2 1

*This is a work of fiction. Any references or similarities
to actual events, real people, living, or dead, or to real
locales are intended to give the novel a sense of reality. Any similarity in other names, characters, places,
and incidents is entirely coincidental.*

Distributed by Kensington Publishing Corp.
Submit Wholesale Orders to:
Kensington Publishing Corp.
C/O Penguin Group (USA) Inc.
Attention: Order Processing
405 Murray Hill Parkway
East Rutherford, NJ 07073-2316
Phone: 1-800-526-0275
Fax: 1-800-227-9604

Acknowledgments

It has been a crazy ride so far. I never thought I would write books, and there are so many people to thank for making it happen.

Momma and Daddy, without you I would be nothing. Thank you for always being there.

My homegirl Marpha, you a trip, girl! You gave me the courage to write, and now look what you've done!LOL.

To my biggest fan, Sue: You give me some of the most amazing inspiration at some of my darkest hours. Ain't no one like you and never will be, girl. You gotta teach me them karate kicks you're famous for.

Katie, you're the best cellie I could ask for. Who knew a white girl could be so down? LOL.

Dan Broccoli, you my boo.

Cushing Hill Gang forever! Still suckin', Hue Grizz!

Urban Books, thanks for believing.

All my girls in lockup, keep ya heads up. They can only keep you down if you let 'em.

To all the corny-ass COs: I'm gettin' paid, suckas.

To my business associates up in Boston: Keep sweepin' it under the rug.

To each and every one of my fans: Thanks for reading and enjoying my stories. I won't stop 'til you had enough. I got nothin' but time.

And last but not least, to God Almighty: Thank you for putting the power of imagination in my head and making it come out through my fingertips.

Chapter 1

Manhunt

"Have you seen this shit?" Mayor Steele showed Dexter Coram, his chief of staff, the headline of the newspaper he was gripping. He was pacing backstage, waiting to go in front of the press and give them an update on the progress of the manhunt for Scar Johnson and Tiphani Fuller—which to this point was nothing.

"Yes, I have, sir." Dexter referred to the headline, which read CITY NOW NEEDS MAYOR TO DISAPPEAR. The article described the disappearance of Tiphani Fuller, a corrupt circuit court judge who had escaped from police custody. As the headline screamed, the newspaper was calling for the resignation of the mayor over this fiasco.

"My opponent is going to jump all over this. These sons of bitches are blaming me for this corrupt bitch." The mayor threw the newspaper on the floor. He was in a tight battle for state senator, and his opponent was gaining ground quickly. This type of damaging headline could be the nail in the coffin for his hopes of election.

"God, I wish I never fucked her," the mayor muttered to himself. It was scaring the shit out of Mayor Steele that Tiphani could come forward at any time with information on their affair. It was the reason he had recommended her in the first place when the governor was looking for someone to promote to circuit judge. Mayor Steele needed to find her and make a deal with her, because if she wasn't willing to cooperate, then she would just have to be taken out permanently.

"We can spin this, sir," Dexter encouraged.

"How?"

"We bring focus back to Scar Johnson and his ambush of the SWAT team."

"Jesus, are you insane? The man is responsible for killing half the SWAT team. How is that better?"

"Well . . ." Dexter had nothing.

Scar Johnson was a notorious criminal in Baltimore. Along with his drug empire, he had been robbing armored cars—with the help of Tiphani Fuller, who just so happened to be sleeping with him—until she started working with the police and tried to set him up. Before they could arrest him, Scar got wind of her deceit and hatched a plan. He intended to kill Tiphani along with the SWAT team. Unfortunately for him, he was only able to take out half the SWAT team, and Tiphani escaped the ambush. Now both Scar and Tiphani were in hiding, and the mayor was left to answer to the public for this failure.

"Damn! Don't we have any new developments to tell these cocksuckers?" the mayor snapped at Dexter.

"No, sir, I'm afraid we don't." Dexter was used to the mayor's outbursts, especially these days.

"Well, fuck it. I'll just have to lead these leeches on and give 'em enough to think we're making progress." With that, the mayor stepped out from behind the stage to begin the press conference.

The energy in the room was palpable. This was the biggest news story to hit Baltimore in a long time. A circuit judge accused of sleeping with and aiding a known criminal to avoid prosecution, and a mayor losing control of his city; it had all the makings of a Hollywood thriller. The members of the press knew they would be getting a lot of mileage out of this story, and their excitement was obvious. As soon as the mayor entered, the cameras clicked all around, as rapid as gunfire, and reporters rushed to pull out their recording devices and notebooks.

"I know you all have a lot of questions, so let's just begin," the mayor announced.

The questions crashed down on him like a tidal wave. Every reporter spoke at once. From the other side of the door, it sounded like an angry mob about to riot. They all wanted their questions to be heard and answered. One female reporter stood up and yelled her question at the top of her lungs. To take some sort of control of the situation, the mayor pointed at her to signal that he would entertain her question first. Seeing this, the rest of the reporters quieted down and let the woman speak.

"Sir, are you any closer to finding Judge Fuller and Scar Johnson, and is there any evidence that they are hiding together?"

"We have many new leads that I am not at liberty to discuss right now."

The mayor was lying. In fact, there were no leads as to the whereabouts of Tiphani or Scar. It was as if they had both disappeared off the face of the earth.

Again the room erupted in questions. The mayor pointed to another reporter.

"Mr. Mayor, Scar Johnson has been terrorizing this city for too long. He killed half the SWAT team, was sexually involved with a circuit judge who presided over his case and set him free, and he is said to have members of the police force on his payroll. Why haven't you done anything about this?"

"I really do not like to dwell on the past," the mayor said weakly. "Let's move forward and focus on the present and why we are all here."

"There is a manhunt for two fugitives who disappeared—a murderous drug kingpin and a judge who escaped from police custody. This is why we are here. What are you doing to keep the citizens safe?" the reporter demanded.

"Again, I am not at liberty to discuss the specifics of our investigation."The mayor appeared calm to the reporters, but inside he wanted to kill every one of them. He had nothing to give them, yet they were just going to keep on pushing with their bullshit questions.

Another reporter yelled out, "Is there anything you can tell us about any new developments?"

"We are working around the clock to bring these two into custody."

"What exactly are you doing?" an obviously irritated reporter asked.

"I have answered that."

"Are you being paid off by Scar Johnson?" someone yelled out.

"Is it true that you had an affair with Judge Tiphani Fuller?"

The questions were coming rapid fire now. They weren't even waiting for him to respond. It was clear that all the reporters were starting to get annoyed with the mayor, who, they suspected, was avoiding questions and not answering truthfully.

"Now we're getting into gossip and slander territory." The mayor jumped in to slow down this line of questioning. The last thing he needed was for it to be printed in the paper that he was screwing Tiphani Fuller and was as corrupt as she was. "If you continue this line of questioning, I will be forced to end the press conference."

***

Scar was sitting on the couch watching the news coverage; his exposed torso still glistening with sweat from the marathon threesome he had just engaged in. He was sandwiched in between two women while the television played the latest on the manhunt for him and Tiphani. The rest of his crew was all hanging around in the other room, cutting and bagging coke. Even though there was a manhunt for Scar, it didn't mean business had to stop. Scar didn't become the most notorious gangster in Baltimore by slacking off and running scared.

During sex, Scar had been distracted, thinking about how the fuck he was going to get out of Baltimore. He was feeling the pressure of the manhunt and was watching the news every chance he got to keep up to date on what the police were doing. So far, no one in his crew or on the street had heard anything that would make them think that the police were close to Scar at all. Still, he wanted to play it safe and stay hidden until he knew for sure he was getting out undetected.

All of Scar's safe houses had been raided, so Scar picked a new safe house that would be the ultimate "fuck you" to the police force; he took over Detective Rodriguez's house. After killing her in the ambush, he thought it only fitting that he should hide out at her house.

Scar was also watching the news to see if there was any information about that bitch Tiphani. He was mad at himself for fucking her. He should have known that any woman who fucks her husband's brother is a snake. Scar loved fucking her, and it turned him on that he was fucking his brother Derek's wife, but the second Tiphani ratted him out to that crooked cop Rodriguez, she sealed her own fate. She was a dead woman in Scar's eyes, and when he finally caught up with that lying, scheming bitch, she would be joining the other lying, scheming bitch Rodriguez in hell.

He had ordered the chief of police to take her out while she was in police custody, but that bumbling fool fucked up everything and let her disappear without a trace. For all Scar knew she could be in Cuba right now, spending all of the money he had stolen from the armored cars and given to her—money that Scar considered his and now wanted back. He wanted to put an end to her trifling ass for good.

"Get out." Scar ordered the two women to leave as the mayor made his appearance on the TV. "I need to watch this alone."

Scar had been violent lately, and the women didn't want to be the ones to get a beating, so without saying a word, they put their clothes on and left the room, no questions asked. As long as Scar provided them with coke, some money, and good dick, they would do whatever he said. It also didn't hurt that they would be out of harm's way in the next room, where all the coke was.

The mayor started his press conference with a brief statement and then took some questions from the press. Scar sat motionless and listened intensely, hoping to read between the lines and figure out what moves the mayor's office was trying to make.

"Yo, Day!" Scar screamed into the next room. "Come here."

When Day entered, he saw Scar sitting back on the couch with one hand in his lap, the other arm draped over the back of the couch, and both eyes glued to the TV.

"What's up?" Day asked.

Without taking his eyes off of the television, Scar said, "Come here and listen to this crooked motherfucker.

Tell me if I'm right and they don't have shit on me. It's like they a chicken with its head cut off, running around in circles with no rhyme, reason, or direction."

Day sat down in a leather recliner. The two of them sat there in silence, watching the mayor give non-answers to the press. He was bobbing and weaving from questions like Muhammad Ali would bob and weave from punches in his prime.

When the press conference ended and the mayor left the podium, Scar picked up the remote and turned off the television.

"What you think?" Scar asked.

"Seems like this nigga don't know shit. I don't think he answered one question. Sounded like if they asked him his name he wouldn't give them a straight answer," Day joked.

"For real, nigga. Don't joke. You think I'm right?"

"In all seriousness, yeah, I think you right. I think if they was close to us, we would know. I got every nigga out there keeping they ears open. We straight," Day said, trying to calm any doubt that might be creeping into Scar's head.

Day needed Scar calm. He needed him in Baltimore. Day wanted revenge on Scar in the worst way, and he didn't want the revenge to be Scar getting picked up by the police. He wanted street justice. He wanted to be the one to take Scar down, just like Scar had been trying to take down Day's mentor, Malek—before Detective Derek Fuller shot him in cold blood. Day was going to make sure they both paid for Malek's death.

Malek was more like an older brother to Day. He had taken Day under his wing and showed him the hustle. Malek was planning to set up shop, make his cash, and then get out. He'd promised to give his operation to Day for his own. Day was getting ready to become a big player in the game, but Scar and Derek put an end to that. Now Day wanted to return the favor.

If Scar got spooked and tried to run without thinking it through, there was a good chance he would get nabbed. The police were pissed and they were working around the clock to find Scar. He had shot and killed several of their own, and when you rattle the nest, the hornets start attacking.

"Stay here until we get the new safe house ready," Day continued. "In the meantime, you worry about the business and stayin' on top. I'll worry about keepin' you outta the eyes of the police."

"You right. They can't touch me! I'm Scar mutha-fuckin' Johnson! I'm the new Teflon Don. I got more than nine lives; I got hundreds," Scar boasted as his face contorted into an evil grin, the scar on his cheek making him look even more sinister.

"What's the word with this bitch Tiphani? Don't seem like the police know anything. What do we know?" Scar asked.

"To be honest, I don't know, boss. Sticks was handling that for you. I didn't really get on top 'cause I was lettin' him do his thing. Seem like he ain't handlin' his business right." He wanted to make sure that Sticks got the blame for it. This was all playing into his plan to disrupt the organization from the inside.

"You need to start knowing, nigga. I need you on top of all of it." Scar was a little agitated with Day.

"Yo, Sticks!" Scar shouted into the other room before Day had a chance to respond and defend himself.

Immediately, Sticks popped into the room, almost as if he had been standing directly on the other side of the door, waiting like an eager puppy to be let into the house.

"What the fuck, nigga? I barely finished saying your name and you standing in front of me." Scar had a disgusted look on his face.

"I was just walking by the room when you called."

"Whatever. Don't be lying and tryin' to eavesdrop like some bitch. You find out where Tiphani is yet?"

Normally Scar would have shot a nigga for acting like that, but right now he needed Sticks alive and on his side. Scar didn't like Sticks and thought he might be gunning for his throne, but he was a businessman and knew that Sticks was willing to do shit none of his other crew would. Sticks was wild and would murk a nigga in a second. So, Scar had to put up with him for now, but kept him at arm's length while keeping an eye on the shifty nigga.

"Nah. After she escaped from the back of the chief's car nobody has seen hide nor hair of that snake bitch. I mean, she still got to be in B-more. With all the roadblocks the cops set up, there ain't no way she got through. If she in B-more, I'll find her." Sticks added a little bravado at the end.

It seemed to Sticks like he constantly had to prove himself to Scar. Sticks had been loyal to Scar since he was a young buck, and he was feeling less than appreciated lately. Scar seemed to be hiding shit from him, and it was starting to really piss Sticks off.

It used to be Timber and Trail that were Scar's main dudes. Sticks was jealous of their position, so he did what he had to do and took those niggas out. After they disappeared, Sticks just played it up to Scar that they were disloyal to him. He thought that after he murked Timber and Trail he would be the main dude Scar turned to for advice, but that shit didn't happen. This punk bitch Day started hounding up on Scar.

Sticks was over this disrespect and was feeling like he could run the crew better himself. He needed to start getting support from some of the new young bucks in the crew and then maneuver his way to the top spot. If that meant deading some niggas along the way, so be it. If that meant going toe to toe with Scar, even better.

"Well then, do it. Find her. Do what you get paid for, nigga. Bring her to me," Scar snapped at Sticks.

"Don't worry. I'm gonna smoke that bitch out of hiding," Sticks replied, trying to keep Scar's confidence in him.

"It ain't gotta be that hard. We got the bitch's kids. When I was fuckin' her on my yacht, she kept talkin' the whole time 'bout how much she missed her kids. Well, I bet she really misses them now," Scar said with a smirk. "As a matter of fact, let's get them little rugrats in here."

He turned his head and yelled, "D.J., Talisa, get your little butts in here."

A few seconds later, the door opened and in came Scar's niece and nephew.

Addressing Scar by his birth name, his seven-year-old nephew said, "Yes, Uncle Stephon?"

"Get your butts over here and give your uncle a hug." Scar softened at the sight of the two young children.

The children ran over to their uncle and Scar scooped them up in his big arms. The kids had been with Scar since he took them the night he ambushed Tiphani, Rodriguez, and the SWAT team. It was easy for Scar to get the kids to come with him since he was their uncle. He just told them that their mommy was on vacation and he was going to take care of them for a while. They loved their uncle and thought he was fun, so they easily went along.

Scar's thinking that night was that he was going to kill Tiphani, take her kids, and then use them as leverage to control their father—who just happened to be Scar's brother. Well, Tiphani escaped death, but he still got her kids and could use them to force his brother Derek, who was a cop, to help him escape from Baltimore. One thing he didn't plan was that the kids would be so damn cute. They were the only people in Scar's life that he could genuinely trust. Their love for him was the only unconditional love Scar had felt ever since he was placed in foster care at the age of four. This clouded his judgment when it came to them. He wanted to use them and toss them like every other person in his life, but he wasn't sure if he would be able to do that to them. His emotions might get in the way.

Day and Sticks both stood there feeling a little uneasy. Neither one of them had ever seen any softness in Scar whatsoever, so standing there while he showed this softer side made them uncomfortable. They were actually afraid that if Scar realized he was being watched while letting his tough demeanor fade, he would lash out with double the usual venom and they would be the recipients. It was not something either one wanted to experience.

Despite their uneasiness, though, they both took note, thinking that they may be able to use this weakness against him later. Day not only wanted to destroy Scar physically, but also mentally, and this might be one way to make Scar feel the mental anguish that he felt when Malek was killed. Even though Sticks didn't care if the little shits lived or died, he wanted to take everything that Scar had, and seeing Scar's reaction toward the kids made Sticks want them.

"Y'all want some ice cream?" Scar asked his niece and nephew.

"Yeah!" They screamed in unison.

"Yo, Sticks, take these two out for some ice cream."

"You want me babysittin' now?" Sticks wrinkled his face in disgust.

"No. I want you to take them out for some ice cream," Scar said methodically as he mean-mugged Sticks. He didn't want to alert the kids to any problems since they were still wrapped up in Scar's muscular arms.

"Why can't Day do it? I got some shit I got to take care of," Sticks replied, sounding like a thirteen-year-old trying to get out of doing his chores.

Scar put the kids down and told them to go and get ready. After they left the room, he spun around and rushed Sticks.

"Muthafucka, don't you be cursing in front of them kids!" Scar got right up in Sticks' face. "When I tell you to do something, you do it. I don't give a fuck what you gotta do. Right now you taking them for some fuckin' ice cream. I oughta bust you in the jaw for that shit." Scar was heated and looked like he was about to go ballistic.

Day was standing there watching the drama escalate, and he jumped in to calm the situation. He wanted to make Sticks look like an ass as well.

"Yo, yo, yo! Chill. I'll take 'em. It ain't all that," he said, trying to get between the two. It was useless, since by this point they were nose to nose.

After a few seconds of silently staring at each other, Sticks gently backed away from Scar. "No, no. You right. My shit can wait. I'll take them little ones for ice cream. It's all good," he said, while in his head he was screaming, *Fuck you, nigga! I should murk your ass right here and now!*

"That's right. You will." Scar turned his back on Sticks and returned to the couch to watch the news coverage.

Sticks wanted so bad to pop Scar, but he knew he needed to make sure that some of the crew would have his back. If he were to kill Scar right now, most niggas in the crew would retaliate and dead his ass for doing so. He was going to have to play this smooth. It would take some time and planning, but Sticks was more determined now than ever before. This disrespect was the last straw. Making a nigga babysit was some disrespectful, punk-ass shit. Before he did something that wouldn't be in his best interest, Sticks thought it best if he got out of there.

"Ay yo, I'ma go." Sticks turned to leave.

"Me too, boss." Day said.

"Wait."

Both Day and Sticks stopped in their tracks. Sticks was thinking, *What the fuck this nigga want now?* Day was thinking, *Oh fuck. What?*

"Day, you stay with me," Scar said, still looking at the television.

This almost sent Sticks into a full-on rage. He was furious that Day was getting special treatment over him. He thought to himself, *I'ma do both these niggas!* He played it cool and stayed calm on the outside, while his insides were erupting like a volcano. Without saying another word, he left to get ice cream.

After Sticks left the room, Scar waited a minute or two and then had Day make sure he wasn't eavesdropping. Day opened the door and saw no signs of Sticks. He figured Sticks was furious but wouldn't be stupid enough to stay and listen. He was probably halfway to the ice cream parlor by now.

"No sign of him, boss," Day reported.

"Something ain't right with that nigga. He on edge. I want you to watch him. Ever since Trail been missing, I ain't trusted his ass," Scar calmly said, looking off into space like he was trying to figure it out in his own head as he was saying it.

"Whatever you want," Day agreed.

Chapter 2

Back from the Dead?

Immediately following the press conference, the mayor went to his office and gathered his staff for an emergency meeting. With his campaign for state senator in danger of spiraling out of control, and his struggle to keep order in the city, the mayor was in desperate need of some good news. He was hoping that one of his staff members would deliver it.

The mayor sat behind his large oak desk and watched as the members of his staff entered the spacious office. Everyone took their respective places, and the mayor leaned back in his leather chair and surveyed the room. They just sat there staring at the mayor, waiting for him to say something. The longer no one said anything, the more nervous the staff started to become. With the tension and confusion mounting, Dexter Coram finally broke the ice.

"Well, I think that went well," the ever positive chief of staff began.

Everyone in the room could feel the collective sigh of relief as the tension was finally released. Following Dexter's lead, the whole staff nodded their heads in agreement. They all wanted to stay positive and encourage the mayor. To put it plain and simple, their futures depended on the mayor's future. If the mayor lost his job, they would also be losing their jobs.

Truthfully, they knew that before the mayor would allow himself to go down, he would take any one of them down first. In order to save his own ass, he wouldn't hesitate to blame one of his staff for what was going on. Therefore, they all wanted to kiss his ass to avoid becoming the sacrificial lamb.

They had good reason to believe that the mayor would throw any one of them under the bus based on what they saw him doing to Tiphani Fuller. Back in the day, it seemed like Tiphani was always getting special treatment from the mayor, no matter how many times she fucked up a case, or how unprofessional she acted. None of the mayor's staff liked her because they felt that she was a detriment to their office, but the mayor would ignore their pleas to fire her. There were always rumors of an affair between Tiphani and the mayor, but when he went so far as to recommend her for a promotion to the circuit court, that pretty much confirmed it in everyone's eyes. They were sure that he was screwing her.

Now, all of a sudden, when his campaign for state senate was in trouble and he needed a boost in his public perception, Tiphani was being outed as a corrupt judge, and a statewide manhunt was on for her. When it was his career on the line, he had no problem airing her dirty laundry to the world. Obviously the only person the mayor cared about was himself. His actions left the staff feeling like it was every man for himself.

"Oh, you think it went very well, huh? I should fire your ass for saying that," the mayor responded to Dexter. "Does anyone have anything to say? Any information?" The mayor was losing his patience.

After a few more seconds of silence, Chief of Police Hill cleared his throat and finally spoke up. He had hoped to perhaps go unnoticed and get out of this meeting without having to say anything, but that wasn't about to happen. Everyone in the room was staring at him.

"Well, sir, as you know, this is our top priority. All other cases have been put on hold. Everyone on the police force is working overtime to find and capture the two suspects. We have called in every favor we have to every agency in the state to assist us in this manhunt—"

The mayor let out an exasperated sigh. "Yes, I know all of this. Most of this was done on my request. Tell me something I don't know, you imbecile!" His patience was gone.

Knowing the mayor was definitely not going to like what he was about to hear, the chief continued. "That's it, sir. Unfortunately, with all of the manpower and hours we are spending, we have nothing. No trace of either one of the suspects.

"One theory is that they escaped the country together. There were some rumors that Judge Fuller had an overseas bank account, but we can't find any evidence of that." Chief Hill stopped for a second to watch the mayor and gauge any reaction.

Hoping to put some sort of positive spin on it, he continued, "I'm working my men to death on this one. We haven't given up, and we are certain we will come up with something eventually."

This pissed the mayor off. Blood rose to his face and he turned bright red. Then, at the top of his lungs, he started screaming, "Eventually! When the fuck is that going to be? You stupid son of—"

"Mr. Mayor, you have a phone call," his secretary announced over the intercom, interrupting him before he could really lay into Chief Hill.

"Not now, Susan."

"But, sir, he won't stop calling. He says it's extremely urgent."

"I don't care! Take a message!" Mayor Steele screamed into the intercom.

"He told me to tell you it's Derek Fuller calling from prison."

The mayor's day had just gone from bad to worse. All the blood that had rushed to Mayor Steele's face disappeared instantly, and a look of shock swept over his face. He was not expecting to hear that name, especially since he had ordered Derek Fuller murdered and had gotten word that the job had been done. Did the guy he paid to kill Derek lie to him? How was this possible? Was this really Fuller, or someone pretending to be him? The mayor's mind was racing with hundreds of different scenarios.

"Everybody out," he commanded.

Happy to have an excuse to leave and end the mayor's tirade, the whole staff got up and out of the office without any hesitation. Being around the mayor right now was a nightmare, and every minute in his presence was just another chance to get screamed at and possibly fired.

As the staff rushed out of the room, the mayor added, "Chief Hill, you can stay in the waiting room. We're not done yet." The rest of the staff was relieved not to hear their names. They were safe from the mayor's wrath for now.

As the door shut after the last staff member exited, the mayor put his hand on the phone receiver, took a deep breath, and picked up the phone.

"Derek!" he said in his most jovial tone, trying to mask the shock he was actually feeling. "How are you? What can I do for you?"

He was cursing himself on the inside for not following up and checking with the prison to confirm that Derek was really dead. He had gotten the phone call saying the job was done, and normally he would have double checked it. With everything going on and being so distracted, he didn't have time and just took the information as fact.

"It's about time you fucking answered! I've been calling, and your bitch secretary wouldn't put me through. I need to get the fuck out of here right now! You promised me weeks ago to get me out. You know I was set up by Scar and I didn't kill Archie. Now, get me out of here!" Derek demanded.

Staying calm, the mayor answered Derek. "Well, I'm not sure how easy that's going to be. I don't know if you've seen the news, but right now I have my hands full with your ex-wife and her lover, Scar Johnson."

"I don't give a fuck!" Derek was starting to sound desperate. "You need to get my ass out of here now! Scar Johnson has threatened my family and tried to have me killed here in prison."

Hearing that put a smile on Mayor Steele's face. Derek thought that the attempt on his life was ordered by Scar, not the mayor. This was the best bit of information the mayor had received in a long time. Even though the attempt on Derek's life didn't work, at least the blame wasn't being put on the mayor. Just to make sure he was in the clear, he wanted to get Derek to clarify. He wanted to be certain there wasn't another attempt on Derek's life that Scar actually did order. So, he asked, "What do you mean, Scar tried to have you killed?"

"There was some fake-ass CO who set me up and stabbed me like forty times. I nearly died. I spent, like, thirty days in the fuckin' hospital ward in ICU before

I finally woke up from a coma. When they found out I was still alive, he sent over one of his boys to threaten me. He told me that if I didn't cooperate and help Scar get out of Baltimore, they would mail my kids' body parts to me one by one."

This phone call kept getting better for the mayor. Not only was he not being blamed for Derek's attempted murder, he just found out that Scar Johnson was still in Baltimore and looking for a way out. At the rate it was going, the case would be solved and the mayor would be guaranteed his senate seat by the end of the call.

"Did they say anything about Tiphani's whereabouts?" the mayor eagerly asked.

"No. I don't care about that deceitful whore. I need to get out of here and rescue my kids!" The urgency in Derek's voice was evident.

"I don't know if that's possible. How will it look if I release the crooked cop husband of the crooked, whoring Justice Fuller? Don't forget, you are in jail for conspiracy and first degree murder. The citizens will have me hung in the town square." The mayor referenced an old custom from medieval times.

"I don't give a fuck! My kids are in danger! You need to find Scar, he needs my help. If I get out, he will find me. Get me out and I will find Scar Johnson. I can also guarantee that Tiphani will appear from the hole she's hiding in." The intensity and desperation from Derek were coming right through the phone.

The mayor remained silent and contemplated this last offer. He was weighing his options. Within this five minute phone call, an incarcerated Detective Fuller had given him more information about Scar than the entire Baltimore police force could. What more would he be able to find out if he was a free man?

As desperate as Derek was to find his kids, the mayor was just as desperate to capture Scar and Tiphani. He needed to take this chance. He would find a way of releasing Derek quietly. If he was lucky, the press would be so consumed with the manhunts that they wouldn't even realize that Derek had been released.

"Okay. Give me a day or two. I'll get you out," the mayor replied.

"Thank you. Thank you. We will get Scar. I promise." A relieved Derek ended the call.

The mayor hung up the phone and leaned back in his chair, thinking, *I hope I don't regret this.*

"Susan, send Chief Hill in here," the mayor said into the intercom.

A moment later, the door to the mayor's office opened and the chief walked in. He was expecting the mayor to pick up where he left off and start screaming at him again. So, to try to stop it before it started, he began to speak immediately.

"Sir, about before . . . we—"

"Sit down, Chief," the mayor interrupted. "I just had an interesting conversation. It seems that this son of a bitch Scar Johnson is still in Baltimore."

A surprised chief asked, "How do you know, sir?"

"Detective Derek Fuller told me. He knows more from prison than your whole police force. Doesn't say much for you or Baltimore's finest, does it?"

"With all due respect, sir, he's a crooked cop. How do you know he's telling the truth?"

"Because he is. You have fucked this whole investigation up. I don't see why I need you around if I can get the answers I need from prisoners. Do you want your job, Chief Hill?"

"Yes, sir, I do. Do you want me to interview Detective Fuller and see what he knows?" Chief Hill felt like he was fighting for his job at this point.

"No. Detective Fuller is going to be quietly released. When he gets out, I want you to know his every move, and after he leads us to Scar Johnson, I want you to kill both of them. Then I want you to find Judge Fuller and kill her too," Mayor Steele calmly ordered.

He wanted Derek dead to make sure he definitely stayed quiet. The mayor couldn't risk Derek revealing that he, the mayor of the city, had struck a deal with a convicted dirty cop who was a cop killer himself.

Chief Hill was stunned. He couldn't tell if the mayor was serious. In order to not get into any more trouble, he decided to stay silent.

"Do you understand? If this doesn't happen, I will personally make sure that you not only lose your job, but that you get publicly humiliated as well. I may even make it look like you were involved with Scar and Tiphani in some way. Hell, you shouldn't have a job right now after you fucked up and let judge Fuller escape," the mayor threatened as he coldly stared at the chief.

"Yes, sir, I understand. I can do that," Chief Hill reluctantly agreed. He was so nervous he didn't even realize that he had been gripping the arms of the chair so tight that he started to put marks in the leather. He was stuck. He had to say yes, and he had to come through. If the mayor went through with his threat, Chief Hill would never be able to get a job again, and even worse, would probably be thrown in jail for conspiracy. He knew that a chief of police in prison would not last very long. Every inmate in the joint would be gunning for his ass so they could make a name for themselves.

"Now, get out of here. I need to figure out how to get Detective Fuller out of jail without the press finding out."

"Yes, sir." Chief Hill was so anxious to leave he practically leapt from the chair. How did he end up in this situation? Another life fucked up by Scar Johnson.

As Chief Hill walked down the corridor of City Hall, he contemplated how he had gotten so involved with Scar. If he hadn't been so greedy and taken those pay-offs, he would be fine. He was thinking he should have killed Scar when he had the chance. Well, now was his chance, and he wasn't going to fuck it up this time. Chief Hill was prepared to kill anyone he needed to in order to keep his position of power—starting with Derek, Scar, and Tiphani.

Chapter 3

Accidental Family

Halleigh walked out of the bedroom and down the hall toward the living room. She had been napping. Between taking care of her son, following members of Scar's crew, and worrying about Dayvid, she wasn't getting much sleep at night. So, any chance she got during the day to catch up on some rest, she did. All of it was wearing her down, but she was determined to follow through with her promise to exact revenge on Scar for the death of her husband, Malek.

After fleeing from Flint, Michigan to start a new life with Halleigh, Malek just wanted a small piece of the streets so he could support his family, but Scar wouldn't allow it. In Halleigh's eyes, Scar was greedy. He could easily have let Malek have his small share and still ruled Baltimore, but instead, Malek ended up dead. So, Halleigh was going to teach Scar a lesson. She was going to teach Scar that greed kills, motherfucker.

As she approached the living room, she heard sounds of cheering coming from not only the people in the room, but from the television as well. She stood in the entryway and leaned against the door frame with her arms crossed in front of her, smiling at what she saw. Sitting on the couch with their backs to her were Dayvid and her son, Malek Jr., watching the Ravens game. She stood there for a few minutes just taking it all in, and it made her happy. To see her baby boy mimicking Dayvid, cheering every time Dayvid did and having such a great time with a positive male role model was the best thing in the world.

Malek Jr. would get extra energy and happiness whenever Dayvid was around. For those few minutes, she forgot about everything else going on in her life and she began to daydream. She started to picture that it was Malek and his son sitting there cheering on their favorite football team while she was in the kitchen cooking dinner for her family. When she snapped out of her daydream and realized Malek wasn't there, she got a little sad. She missed him, and hadn't realized just how much until then. She had been so focused on her revenge plot with Dayvid and taking care of little Malek that she hadn't allowed herself any time to think about the past. Now it all hit her like a ton of bricks.

She thought back to all the events in her life that had led her up to this point, from the moment she met Malek to losing contact with him to being forced into prostitution, and then finally reuniting with Malek. When they had a son and escaped from Flint, Halleigh thought her life was on track to be happily ever after— until Malek was gunned down in their front yard right in front of her. It was all too much for her to handle. If she allowed herself to think about it for too long, she would lose control, and she couldn't afford to do that. She had a beautiful baby boy that she was determined to raise right. She wasn't going to let him make the same mistakes she made in her life.

Malek Jr. was about the same age as Halleigh was when she lost her father. The one thing she wished growing up was to have a dad around the house. She always felt her life would have been so much better if a loving father had been in the picture. Her mom wouldn't have gotten hooked on crack, she wouldn't have had strange men coming in and out of the house all the time, and Halleigh wouldn't have gotten raped by a few of those strange men. She wished now that Malek Jr. could have a loving father in the house, but Scar Johnson and Detective Derek Fuller took that away from him.

"Mommy! They're winning!" Malek Jr. excitedly exclaimed when he saw Halleigh standing behind him.

"I see, baby," she said, breaking out of her own thoughts and putting a smile on her face for her boy.

"Watch. It fun." Malek Jr. scooted closer to Dayvid to make room for Halleigh on the couch.

"Yeah, it's fun. Come watch." Dayvid smiled.

"How about I make you some popcorn first?" Halleigh asked.

Malek Jr. and Dayvid turned to one another with wide eyes and smiles across their faces and gave each other a pound. "Yes!" they both said, not so much as an answer to the question, but as an agreement with each other at how awesome the idea was.

Halleigh chuckled at the sight of Dayvid's big fist and Malek Jr.'s tiny fist bumping into each other.

A few minutes later, Halleigh came back from the kitchen. "Popcorn's ready," she said as she entered the room and sat in the space that Malek Jr. had made for her on the couch.

The three of them sat there eating popcorn and watching football. It was an exciting game that kept them riveted to the action. Somewhere around the middle of the fourth quarter, Malek Jr. starting getting sleepy. He was fighting to stay awake and watch the end of the game. He snuggled his head into his mama's chest as he reached over and grabbed Dayvid's hand.

"I like this," he said as his eyelids became heavier with every passing second.

"You like the game, baby?" Halleigh asked her sleepy little boy.

"No," he replied.

Before Halleigh could even ask what he meant, little Malek was asleep. Halleigh looked down at her now sleeping boy and then over at Day, who was already looking at her. They stared at each other. Halleigh didn't understand what her baby boy was referring to. Then Dayvid said, "I like this too," and grinned.

Suddenly, Halleigh became a little nervous and looked down at her boy in order to break eye contact with Dayvid. His words helped her understand what her little boy meant. It wasn't the game he was referring to; it was the moment. Malek liked everything about that moment—watching football, eating popcorn, and sitting between a man and his mama. To his little mind, it felt like a family—the kind of family Halleigh had been daydreaming about no more than an hour ago.

"I'll take him to bed." Not knowing how to react and already feeling a bit uncomfortable, Halleigh started to gather Malek Jr. in her arms.

"Okay." Dayvid helped her with her son. "Good night, M.J." he said as he kissed the boy on his forehead.

He watched Halleigh carry the boy down the hall and into his bedroom. Even though she was carrying a child in her arms, Dayvid still couldn't help but check out Halleigh's bangin' body. Dayvid had always thought Halleigh was fine, but lately it seemed to him that he was maybe feeling a little more than just sexual attraction to her. He would never say anything to her about it, though. He wouldn't disrespect his deceased friend Malek like that. Besides, he saw how Halleigh just reacted when all he did was agree with her son and say how good it felt to be on that couch with them. She obviously wasn't feeling the same thing that he was.

"Well," Halleigh said as she sat back down on the couch after putting her son to bed. "That little man was out."

"Yeah, he sure was. That little dude is mad fun to watch the game with. He know nothing about what's happenin' on the screen, but he still be rootin'," Dayvid said with a smile on his face.

"Yeah, he's cute," she agreed, trying to decide if she should mention anything about the awkward moment that just happened between them or just leave it.

Dayvid sat there thinking the same thing, but decided he wasn't going to be the one to say anything about it. He just sat there waiting for Halleigh to break the silence. After a few seconds, Dayvid checked the time on his phone.

"I should go. Gotta see Scar and keep up this charade. Don't want him to stop trusting Day," he said, referring to the name that he used with Scar. "I think he's getting paranoid. Seems like he ain't trustin' no one right now. 'Cept me, of course." He finished with a mischievous grin across his face.

"Good. Fuck him." Halleigh pursed her lips. "We should just ice him now. Make it look like the cops did it."

"It ain't that easy. He never leaves his place. I can't make it look like the cops unless he go outside, and that shit ain't happenin'. He playin' it real safe right now."

"I don't know how much longer I can wait." Halleigh was getting impatient and wanted Scar dead now.

"It won't be long. We just have to hold out. He has me stayin' real close to him. It's just a matter of time."

Dayvid was trying to stall Halleigh and keep her satisfied as to the progress of their plan. As he became more
involved in Scar's crew, he started thinking that he could
take over, if not all of the business, at least a part of it. He
saw that he could live a nice life with a piece of that action.
He was afraid that Halleigh wouldn't go for that, so he
kept that part of his plan to himself. Her only focus was
to make Scar suffer while he died. She didn't care about
his money or his empire. In fact, after they had destroyed
Scar, she wanted nothing to do with the streets. Malek
had left her with a nice chunk of change that she could
live on.

"It better be soon," she warned.

"It will, I promise. I gotta go," he said as he put on his
coat and rushed to the door, leaving Halleigh sitting on
the couch.

Chapter 4

Planning my Comeback

The midday Florida sun was shining through the window. Tiphani lay on the bed naked, next to Cecil, with their legs intertwined. They had just finished another one of their marathon fuck sessions. Even with all of the stress in her life, Tiphani was still just as insatiable as ever. She couldn't get enough dick.

Cecil needed a breather. He had never met a woman so sex crazed that she wore him out. It was usually the other way around. He could go on all night, usually ending with the women begging him to stop because they couldn't handle it anymore. But not Tiphani. She was an animal; it was never enough for her. What he didn't know was that Tiphani had other motives. She knew that if she kept fucking Cecil this good, she could probably get him to do whatever she wanted.

Tiphani had ended up here in Florida after escaping from the back of Chief Hill's car in Baltimore. She had run down the road until an understanding truck driver picked her up. Without asking any questions, he let her hide in the back of his cab under some nasty old blankets.

When the driver had to stop at the roadblock leading out of Maryland, the cop who was to check the truck's interior stuck his head inside the window, took one sniff of the funky body odor emanating from the driver, and decided not to investigate any further. The officer was not about to subject his nose to the nastiest stench he had ever smelled for any longer than he had to. He let the driver pass through without searching the truck.

To Tiphani's surprise, the driver never once made a move on her or demanded sex in return for helping her. He was a happily married, churchgoing man, who loved his wife and never once thought of cheating on her. He just wanted to help those in need and never passed judgment on any human. He told Tiphani that he left the judgment up to God and the person's own conscience. He followed in Jesus' teachings and loved all men equally.

The driver transported Tiphani across several state lines, all the way to Fort Lauderdale, Florida. She felt like he was her guardian angel.

The first thing she did in Florida was to make contact with her offshore bank accounts. She needed money to set herself up with a place to stay. She was going to be dealing strictly in cash from here on out. The off-shore bank was more than happy to wire her money. They took the information for the Western Union that Tiphani provided, and within minutes, she had several thousand dollars. Every few days, she would have them send more money, each time to a different location.

Having more than enough to live on, she started in on her plan to get back to Baltimore. She rented an apartment overlooking the water in Fort Lauderdale, bought a computer, and got to work. Every morning, she would catch up on the news coming out of Baltimore. It seemed to her that they were really fucking up and nowhere near finding her or Scar.

Her afternoons were spent searching the databases of all the prisons in the area, carefully researching certain prisoners who were about to be released. She had a plan, and she would need someone with some special skills. The easiest place she could think to find someone like that was in the prison system.

When she would find a prisoner who seemed like he might be a candidate, she would go to the prison to visit as a lawyer. She had some fake IDs and fake business cards made up, which made it easy for her to go in and out of the prisons. Tiphani would visit under the premise that she was a defense attorney looking to do pro bono work. She would say she thought that there might be grounds to sue the government on behalf of the prisoner, due to a technicality in their case. Little did the prisoners know that it was basically one big audition to see if they fit in with what Tiphani needed.

After a while, Tiphani was becoming frustrated. There had been several prisoners she made contact with, but none were good enough. One was just too damn stupid and would never be able to help her, one had clearly turned into a punk and was now some other inmate's bitch and was too worried about looking pretty, and one was so butt ugly that she couldn't stand to look at him for even a second. She was starting to think that she would have to move her search to another state.

This wasn't what she wanted to do. Moving around too much and crossing state lines would give more people an opportunity to recognize her. Finding another apartment to rent where the owner would be willing to accept cash with no questions might not be as easy. She was taking a huge risk already, and with her escape being national news, Tiphani knew visiting prisoners wouldn't be safe for much longer.

She decided she would give her search through the Florida prison system one last chance before coming up with a new plan—and she was happy she did.

Deciding to go back through prisons she'd already researched proved to be fruitful. She locked on to one prisoner in particular that looked on paper like the perfect candidate. He was a former Army sergeant who was in prison for aggravated assault and about to be released.

When Tiphani first laid eyes on Cecil, she got wet between her legs. He was six foot four of pure muscle, bald and full of confidence. His eyes were what really made him stand out. Not only were they the perfect almond shape, but they each had their own color. His left eye was light hazel, and his right eye was dark brown. Tiphani realized this must be why he had the nickname Twotone.

He walked in the empty interview room and his energy immediately filled the space. The way the guards were reacting to him, he obviously commanded their respect. She knew right away that she had found her man.

He sat down across the metal table from her and looked directly into her eyes. She felt like he could see right through her into her soul. She shivered a bit, but immediately composed herself and went into lawyer mode. She shuffled a few papers around before she began. He stayed silent and just watched her with suspicion.

She folded her hands in front of her on the table and began. "So, you know why I am here?"

"I know why you say you're here."

"Good. So I don't need to go into specifics."

"I think you do." Cecil looked her right in her eyes as if he were daring her to convince him.

"Okay. I see you're a man who demands all the facts before making a decision." She then proceeded to tell the same bullshit story she told to every other prisoner she had interviewed.

Cecil continued staring at her as he remained silent. His apparent self-confidence was turning Tiphani on, but also throwing her off.

"Well, ah, I was a . . ." She reached down and fumbled with her briefcase that sat on the floor beside her chair and pulled out some folders. Cecil still said nothing.

Tiphani continued, "I was, ah, looking through some files of some old cases, and yours was of particular interest to me." She placed a file on the table in front of her.

"Why?" Cecil asked.

"Well, I am doing pro bono work."

"That doesn't answer my question. Why is my case interesting to you?"

"I believe very much in justice, and in your case, I think there has been great injustice. There seems to be some discrepancies in your case and in the evidence provided against you."

"Like what? Can I see my file you have in front of you?"

"Oh, this is confidential material, and I can't show you unless we actually start working together." She put the folder back in the briefcase. "There are many things that interested me about your case, but I don't want to get into specifics right here. You never know who could be listening." Tiphani whispered the last sentence and gave a flirtatious smile.

"We are in this room alone. No one is listening but me. Tell me about these discrepancies." Cecil still had not averted his eyes from Tiphani.

"Okay. I believe some of the evidence might have been tampered with. Some of the testimony given was perhaps false. There are other things, but now is not the time to go into all of that. I am here to speak with you about your side of the story. I want to take this case when you are released, which I believe is going to be soon. Am I right? I just want reassurance from you that you will be in it one hundred percent once we start going forward with the lawsuit. I can foresee a big payday for you. "

Her story was well rehearsed, and to someone not versed in the law and not paying close attention, it would sound legitimate. All of the other prisoners bought into it, but not Cecil. He was skeptical. Her story didn't sound right to him. It sounded too rehearsed and unnatural. This was perhaps because he had made her nervous and flustered and had thrown her off her game. The entire time she was giving her speech, she couldn't stop imagining riding his dick.

"So, what do you think?" she asked.

"Sounds like bullshit to me."

"I assure you it's not."

"Look, stop lying. Why are you really here? Did someone send you?"

Tiphani thought for a second. How else could she come at him? *Let's try a different approach*, she thought.

"What did you do in the Army?"

"Explosive Ordinance Disposal. E.O.D. specialist. Is that why you are here? I don't have time for this." He turned to call the guard.

Tiphani knew it was no use in trying to keep up the lie. He was too smart to fall for her story, and besides, he had her way off her game.

"Wait. I'll tell you why I'm really here." She paused, looked down to stall for time so she could think up something. Nothing was coming. He waited a few moments then turned again for the guard.

"I wanted to meet you," she blurted out.

"Why?"

"Honestly?I saw your picture and I thought you were fine. I was hoping that we might get together when you get released." It was the first thing that came to her head. Anyway, it was based in truth; it wasn't all a lie.

"You sayin' you want to fuck me when I get out?"

Her knees got weak. She got hot all over, and she was speechless for a moment. "Yes."

"Why should we wait 'til I get out?"

Tiphani said nothing. She wasn't sure what he was saying. She thought she knew, but she wasn't sure.

"Let's see how fine you think I am." He got up from his seat and walked over to the guard. They exchanged a few whispered words and then the guard stepped out of the room.

Cecil walked back over to Tiphani and stood next to her chair. She remained silent and turned her head toward him. He placed his hand on her chin and lifted her face so their eyes met.

"If you want to fuck, then let's fuck," he propositioned.

She slowly stood up from her chair like she was in a trance. When she stood fully erect, time briefly stood still; then they started kissing each other. Cecil didn't waste any time. He pulled Tiphani's skirt above her waist, ripped open her stockings, and yanked her panties off. With her pussy exposed, Cecil spun her around and powerfully bent her over the table. He pulled down his pants, unleashed his dick, and forcefully plunged into her.

She gasped at the abruptness of it, but took it all in. She loved it. She hadn't been fucked like this since she was with Scar.

"Fuck me hard."

He pounded into her with authority. He had complete control over her. She was pushing back, trying to get every last inch of him.

"Oh yeah, daddy. Spank me."

He obliged by smacking her ass several times, leaving hand prints. He spread her ass cheeks and continued his assault.

The harder the better was Tiphani's motto. She needed this.

Finally, Cecil pulled out of her with a groan and shot his cum all over her ass. She reached around and wiped it all up then licked it off her hand. She stayed bent over the table with her arms and legs spread out until he told her to get up.

"Is that what you wanted to do when I got out of here?"

"Mmmm. That was better than I could have dreamed."

"Give me your card. I'll holla at you when I'm sprung."

She pulled her skirt down then took a business card from her briefcase.

"You can call me at this number. It's my private cell." She wrote her number on the back of her fake business card. He took it and walked to the door and had the guard let him out. She composed herself, gathered her things, and left shortly after.

Cecil "Twotone" White was released a little over a week later. He called her the second he stepped foot outside of Everglades Correctional Institution. She picked him up drove him back to Fort Lauderdale, and they hadn't been away from each other yet.

Now, here they were, naked and in bed, the place they spent most of their time. When they were hungry, Tiphani would either order in or send Cecil out to get food. She didn't see the need to take the chance to go outside and be recognized. She was happy to stay inside, get fucked, and begin her psychological breakdown of Twotone.

Tiphani figured it was time to put her plan in motion. She got up from the bed and stood in front of the window that looked out over the ocean. Standing there naked, with her arms crossed in front of her, she took in a deep breath and let out a heavy sigh.

Cecil rolled over when he heard the sigh. "What's wrong, baby?"

This is too easy, she thought. "Nothing."

"Something's on your mind. Tell me."

Like an Oscar-winning actress, she took a dramatic pause, kept staring out the window, and let a few tears fall from her eyes. "It's just . . ." Another pause. "I'm thinking of my children." Tiphani had yet to tell Cecil anything about her past. This was the first he was hearing anything about children.

"You have kids? Where are they?"

"They were taken from me."

Cecil propped himself up on his elbows. "By who? What do you mean?"

She turned to him with tears in her eyes. Her act was pulling him in. It was much easier than she had expected. *Maybe I should be an actress,* she thought then quickly got back on track. She was going in for the kill now. She was going to tug on his heartstrings.

"I have a confession to make. Promise you won't be mad."

"Of course not. Tell me." She had his full attention now.

"I have a past that I haven't told you about."

"We all do."

"Mine is complicated and twisted."

"Can't be any worse than mine. I'm a convict," he joked, trying to lighten her mood.

She smiled a bit to let him know she got his little joke.

"Well, first I want to tell you I'm down here hiding, and that I'm wanted by the law."

"So you're not a lawyer?"

"No, I am a lawyer. In fact, I'm a judge, but I was set up, and now they're looking for me. See, I was married to a man, Detective Derek Fuller—he's the man I had my children with. We had a fine marriage, except for one problem. He was awful in bed. I mean, he was the worst fuck ever. He was the ultimate minute man. Heck, I was lucky if he lasted a minute.

"Anyway, he has a brother, Scar Johnson, who is a major drug dealer in Baltimore. Those two don't get along. Well, they did get along, until Derek thought that Scar was fucking me."

Tiphani looked Cecil in the eyes to reinforce this next lie. "He wasn't." She paused to see if Cecil believed her. He seemed to, so she proceeded. "I thought he was just being a good brother-in-law and listening to my frustrations about my husband. Little did I know he was using me so I would help him in his trial and keep him out of prison. I was so gullible." She looked to Cecil with puppy-dog eyes to gain his sympathy.

"So, after Scar avoided jail, he turned on me. I think he and the mayor started working together to ruin my career and my life. Somehow, they made up a tape that sounded like Scar and I having sex and played it for the whole city of Baltimore to hear." She started crying.

"Wait, why would the mayor do anything like that? And why would he work with a drug dealer? For that matter, why would Scar turn on you? You're his brother's wife." Cecil became skeptical of this tale.

Tiphani sniffled and wiped her tears. She took a second to compose herself and think of how she could explain all of this and still look like she was just a victim.

"I walked in on the mayor fucking one of the district attorneys. He's been having an affair with her for years. He kept sending his chief of staff, Dexter, this squirrely creep with hairy ears, to threaten me and keep me quiet. He probably worked with Scar because I'd just set him free. They probably worked out some deal and made the tape so I would look like a corrupt judge. Scar wanted me out of the picture because he thought I turned on him."

Pretending that she was about to break down again, she took a deep breath like she was gathering her emotions and continued. This was turning into a masterful acting job. "He thought I was ratting him out for robbing armored cars, but I was just talking with my friend, who happened to be a detective. Next thing I know, he killed her then came after me, but I escaped—not only once, but twice.

"When I got arrested for corruption, the police chief came and said he was transferring me, but I knew better. He was going to kill me. I wriggled out of the handcuffs and jumped out of the back of his moving car and ran away. Some trucker picked me up and drove me here to Florida."

"What about your husband?" Cecil was trying to keep everything in this story straight. So far it seemed legit to him.

"He was threatening to kill me too. He ended up going to jail for murder. He killed the entire unit he was in charge of. I knew he wasn't the straightest cop out there, especially since he had a drug dealing brother, but I didn't think he would resort to murdering his friends. I'm such a fool." She broke down in tears and heaving sighs of woe. "My kids were kidnapped and now are God knows where. They had nothing to do with anything."

"These crooked mu'fuckas." Cecil slowly shook his head in disbelief. He was getting angry at the injustice he thought had been done to Tiphani.

Cecil hugged her with his massive arms. He tried to calm her down by stroking her hair and rubbing her back. She continued to sob. She wasn't about to stop this act now.

"I just want my children back and for them to be safe. I don't know what to do. I'm wanted, I have no friends left, and I'm not strong enough to fight them," she said through more tears and heaving sobs.

"You have me."

She looked up at him with those same puppy-dog eyes. "Really? My story doesn't scare you away?"

"Hell no."

She kissed him. "I'm afraid. I don't know how to go up against those men." Now she was playing to his manly ego.

He took it bait, line, and sinker. "I have a few ideas. I can help you, girl."

"You mean it? You'll help me?"

"I will do whatever it takes to get those kids back for you and to take revenge on all those mu'fuckas."

She hooked him. She couldn't believe how easy it actually was. She guessed it was true that men think with their dicks. To reward him for being so kind and gullible, Tiphani started kissing her way down his chest to his dick and gave him head.

Chapter 5

Man against Man

"Where the fuck you been?" Scar asked Day as he walked in the room.

"Watching the Ravens game." As always, Day had his alibi down pat.

"Why you ain't watch it here, nigga? I got the high-def flat screen." Scar gestured with pride to his sixty-inch television.

"I watched it at Friday's. You know I be tryin' to fuck the bartender there." Day continued his alibi.

"What's his name?" Sticks punked Day.

"What?"

"What the dude's name you tryin' to smash?" Sticks said with a smirk on his face.

Day instantly went after Sticks. "I'm gonna knock you the fuck out!" he barked as he charged toward Sticks. He wasn't going to let Sticks disrespect him like that. Day was going to make him shut his mouth with a hook to the jaw.

Before Sticks could do anything, Day was on him, but Sticks blocked the wild punch that Day threw. Sticks grabbed Day by the neck, and the struggle for control was on.

"Back the fuck up, punk!" Sticks screamed as he pushed Day backward. He pulled his gun from his waistband and pointed it at him.

"Fuck you! You the punk pulling your piece in a fist fight," Day shot back.

Bang! A gunshot went off inside the room. The argument immediately stopped and the room fell silent. Almost instantly, the door to the room was kicked in, and storming through the door came three of Scar's crew, with guns drawn, ready to blast.

"Drop yo mu'fuckin' gun, nigga!"

"Drop yo piece!"

"Drop that shit!"

They were all screaming and pointing their guns at Sticks when they saw him standing there with his gun drawn.

"Yo, chill, my li'l niggas. Chill! It's cool!" Scar yelled over all of their screams.

Everyone turned their attention to Scar and saw him standing there holding a gun at his side. He had fired his gun into the ceiling to put an end to the fight.

"Yo, Scar, we heard a gunshot." Flex, one of the newest members of the crew, said. He had gotten his name because he was so jacked it looked like he was always flexing his muscles.

"I was trying to keep these two fools from killing each other," he said, pointing with his gun in the direction of Day and Sticks. "It's all good. You on point coming in here like the mu'fuckin' cavalry, yo."

"We got yo' back. Whenever. Bet," Flex said as he gestured with his head for the other two to follow him out the door.

Scar turned to Day and Sticks. "Now, you two mu'fuckas stop acting like bitches. Put yo' gun away."

Sticks complied and put his gun back in his waistband. "I was just joking around. Who knew this nigga was so sensitive?" he said. "Unless the truth hurts." Even though he was joking, he knew it would piss Day off.

This last little remark pushed Day over the edge again. He had put up with Sticks' bullshit long enough. It was time this nigga got taught a lesson for real. He was going to break his jaw so he couldn't talk any more shit.

"Fuck you!" Day started toward Sticks again.

"Enough!" Scar wolfed out, which stopped Day in his tracks. "This shit is dead now! Now, sit the fuck down, both of you."

They both hesitated, and then obeyed like children who just got scolded.

Scar lectured the two. "I'm not gonna make you two hug it out or any corny shit like that. You both men, so handle it like men. We all want the same thing, mad paper, so let's make that shit. We don't need to be fightin' like bitches."

"Word," they both mumbled, but this was far from over. Neither Sticks nor Day were about to drop it. They both sat there, already plotting out ways to murk each other.

Scar stayed standing in front of the two. He stared at them with a look of disgust and confusion on his face. He couldn't understand why niggas were so stupid and childish sometimes.

"We have a new safe house yet? I'm sick of staying inside this place all the damn time. I might as well be in the joint."

"I got my man looking for a place in that nice part of northern Baltimore County. We be lookin' for, like, an estate. Mad land for you to walk around on. You won't have to leave yo' property," Day said. In reality, he was stalling. He hadn't been looking for a place at all. He thought it would be easier to keep an eye on Scar if he stayed in Baltimore.

"Nigga, you sound like a real estate agent. Just get it done." Scar was scowling.

"Yo, one problem, though." Sticks wanted to be involved as well.

"What?" Scar asked

"The cops still have mad roadblocks up. This city is on lockdown. It might be risky," Sticks warned.

"Fuck," Scar said under his breath as he began to slowly pace. He was trying to figure out a way to get out of Baltimore risk free. Sticks was right; it was risky without knowing exactly when and where they would be stopping cars. Though he didn't want to do it, he figured the best way would be to get Chief Hill on board. After the fiasco with Tiphani, Scar was reluctant to ask the chief to do anything else. He couldn't have fucked that up any worse. Scar had told the chief to take Tiphani out of the city, shoot her, and stash the body; but he somehow let her escape from the back of his car and disappear.

"Sticks, go talk to the fuckin' idiot chief and tell him he needs to help us." Scar was unsure if this was really the best idea, but felt he had no other choice.

"Word? I'll do it now." Sticks stood up. He was eager to get the hell out of that room. The whole time he was sitting there, all he wanted to do was bitch-slap Day and murk his ass. He was happy to go speak to the chief and show Scar he was capable of doing his business. Day seemed to be fucking up with the safe house, so it was a perfect time for Sticks to step up. He wanted to be close to Scar to learn everything he could about his empire. Then when he took Scar down, he could triple the operation.

"Not yet. I need to tell you what to say. Chill for a minute," Scar said.

"You want me to go with him? It would be more intimidating with the both of us," Day asked.

"Nah. You two need to be separate for right now. Sticks got this. You get that safe house in order," Scar said.

"A'ight. Whatever you say, boss." Day played the good soldier, but on the inside he was pissed. He wanted to go so he could get an angle on the chief for himself.

Scar just stood there staring at Day, waiting for him to get up and go. "What the fuck? Don't be sittin' there. I'm sick of being up in this bitch. These walls are pissin' me off. I mean now. Find me a new place."

"Oh yeah, right. I'll take a drive north and see what's happening." With that, Day got up and out the door.

After Day was gone, Scar turned to Sticks, who was sitting down rolling a blunt.

"Stop that for a second and listen to me," Scar ordered.

Sticks stopped rolling the blunt and leaned back on the couch. "What you need? What you want me to say to the chicf?"

"I'll get to that. First thing, I want you to keep an eye on that nigga Day. Something don't feel right. I ain't never seen him with a bitch, and now he talkin' about fuckin' some bartender," Scar said as he twisted his lips.

"A'ight, I can do that. I feel you. Something off about that nigga. I can murk that nigga if you want. You know I ain't got a problem with that," Sticks said, hoping the answer would be yes. He was definitely sick of the attention Day was getting and was happy that Scar was questioning him. If Scar gave him the go ahead, Sticks thought it would make his life so much easier.

"Not yet. He still my nigga. I just need to know what's up," Scar said.

That was not the answer Sticks wanted to hear. Sticks knew what was up. Day was a kiss-ass who needed to be murked.

"Now, roll that blunt," Scar said as he sat on the couch. He was going to get these two to play against each other. In his mind, it was a masterful plan that would keep both of them in line and on his grind for a while. He would keep flipping the script on them. One day he would favor Sticks, then the next he would favor Day; make them each think he wasn't really feeling the other one. If they both thought they had a chance, then they would be trying to outdo each other. When they would see the other getting more attention, they would then work harder and be more loyal soldiers. Scar thought of it as a type of psychological warfare.

Chapter 6

Follow the Money

Chief Hill sat in his car in the parking lot, replaying the events that happened earlier in the day. After Hill's morning meeting with the mayor, Sticks had approached the chief in front of City Hall. It was a risky move by Sticks. He knew every agency in Baltimore was searching for Scar, and since he was a known associate of Scar, they would probably be looking for him as well. He didn't give a fuck, though. Sticks wanted to send a message to the chief that he wasn't scared. He also wanted to make a point to Flex that he was a real nigga, not afraid of shit.

Flex and Sticks had been in a car outside of the massive marble building, waiting for the chief to appear. After about an hour, the chief finally came walking out of City Hall. Sticks stayed in the passenger's seat and watched Chief Hill descend the steps and head down the street toward his car.

Sticks came up behind him before he could open his car door.

"Ay yo," Sticks said, standing on the sidewalk. The car created a barrier between them. Chief Hill looked up and knew right away who the person standing on the opposite side of his car was, but acted as if he didn't. They had met plenty of times before, while Chief Hill was receiving bribe money from Scar.

"Can I help you?" he asked.

"We need to talk," Sticks replied.

Still acting confused, the chief furrowed his brow. "I'm sorry. I don't believe I know you."

"Stop fuckin' around, nigga. You know who I am and why I'm here." Sticks was putting an end to the chief's little charade. He wanted to get on with it and get out of there. Even if he wanted to act like he wasn't scared, Sticks knew that standing in front of City Hall wasn't the safest place for him to be at the moment.

The chief slowly looked around, trying not to draw attention to himself while he searched for anyone who might be watching them. The last thing he needed right now was to be caught speaking with a known associate of Scar Johnson. Satisfied that no one was watching them, he turned back to Sticks.

"Where is Scar?" he asked in a hushed tone.

"Don't worry about that. You and me is gonna talk. Let me in your car."

"No. Not here and not without Scar."

"Nigga, that ain't happenin'. We talkin', and if we don't, you gon' be sorry," Sticks warned.

The chief knew that Sticks' threat was credible. After years of working with Scar and taking his money, the chief saw firsthand what Scar was capable of doing. He also figured that if he played along, he could get to Scar and do as the mayor wanted—find him, kill him, and put an end to his stranglehold on the city.

"Meet me at midnight at the twenty-four-hour diner up on I-95," Chief Hill directed.

Sticks had met the chief at that diner plenty of times to give him his bribe money, so he knew exactly where he was talking about. It was far enough outside of the city that they wouldn't be recognized, and it was just dirty enough that no one really gave a fuck about anything. They could meet there, conduct their business, and not be bothered by anyone.

"A'ight. If you don't show, it's yo' head. Don't be tryin' to set me up, neither."

"Bring Scar." The chief gave an attempt to get Scar out of hiding.

Ignoring the chief's request, Sticks said, "Just be there at midnight." And with that, Sticks walked away, leaving the chief standing at his car.

Snapping out of his replay, Chief Hill looked at his watch. It was 11:55 P.M., five minutes until he was supposed to meet Sticks—and hopefully, Scar. He reached over, opened the glove compartment, and removed the Glock .45 GAP. He took the gun and tucked it in the waistband of his pants. He wasn't going to take any chances with this meeting. If Scar showed up, he might just try to shoot him on the spot.

Even if Scar didn't show up, he thought Sticks might try to set him up, which was why he got to the diner an hour early. He wanted to stake it out and make sure there was no one waiting to ambush him. With it being so close to the meeting time and none of Scar's crew seemingly anywhere in sight, he figured he wasn't about to be ambushed.

While he sat there waiting for the final five minutes to pass, he gave one last look around the parking lot. It seemed clear to him, so he got out of the car, walked across the parking lot and into the diner.

After their encounter with the chief, Sticks had Flex drop him off and then go immediately to the diner. Sticks wanted Flex to make sure the police didn't set up any sort of trap. Flex had picked up a nondescript Nissan Maxima at a chop shop and put out-of-state plates on it so it wouldn't stick out at the roadside diner. Flex had been in the parking lot ever since. He had been sitting in the backseat of the car all day.

He had watched Chief Hill drive and walk around the parking lot a few times and then sit in his car the rest of the time. When Chief Hill would get anywhere near his car, Flex hid under a blanket on the floor. The tinted windows made it difficult for the Chief to see inside, so he didn't inspect it as carefully as the other cars in the lot.

Watching from the back seat through the dark tint windows, it didn't seem to Flex that the chief was planning on any trap. If anything, it looked to Flex like the chief was searching for a trap that might be set for him. When the hour passed and the chief walked into the diner, Flex called Sticks on his throw-away cell phone.

"Yo, he's just goin' in now. Everything look good."

"Good lookin', my nigga. I'll be there in a minute. Just chill there; make sure nothin' goes down. I'm gonna reward you nice for your work," Sticks answered, feeling good. He had found the crew member he was going to groom and get on his side. Flex would be the first one Sticks would recruit when he started forming his own crew. Sticks' plan was to start giving Flex jobs like this one and pay him enough cash to keep him wanting more. That way Sticks could convince Flex that he could make more money with him and not Scar.

Sticks, who had been parked at a rest stop about a mile away, ended the call and made his way to the diner. A few minutes later, he pulled into the parking lot, parked his Escalade, and walked into the diner.

As he was entering the diner, Sticks saw the finest girl he'd seen in a while heading to the entrance as well. She had all the right curves in all the right places, and she wore clothes that accentuated them perfectly. Day couldn't take his eyes off her firm breasts and round, perfect ass.

She saw him looking and gave her ass an extra little bounce as she walked. Day sped up his walk so he could reach the door at the same time as she did. She reached for the door, but Sticks beat her to it.

"Let me get that for you, ma." He opened the door for her and seductively looked into her eyes.

She matched his gaze with an equally seductive look of her own. "What a gentleman."

"Anything for a fine young woman as yourself."

"Manners, charming, and sexy. I think I like you." She winked at him and walked into the restaurant, making sure he had a nice view of what she knew he wanted—her ass.

"Yo, ma. Let me holla at you."

"You want my number?" She batted her eyelashes and played coy. She knew this game all too well.

"That ain't all I want." He rubbed his chin.

"Ooh, and a sense of humor. I definitely like you." She reached in her Gucci purse and pulled out a pen and paper.

Sticks looked around the restaurant and saw Chief Hill staring at him, so he cut their encounter short. He wanted to keep pushing up on this chick, because she seemed down to fuck. If he kept working on her, she'd be fucking him in the bathroom in no time. But he had business that couldn't wait.

"I'ma definitely holla at you real soon." Sticks took her number.

"I hope so." She grabbed his hand and looked in his eyes one last time.

Sticks got so turned on he practically busted a nut right there. He turned and headed straight for the back booth, where the chief was already waiting.

With no emotion showing on his face at all, Sticks sat down across from Chief Hill. He was trying to get his mind off that woman. He needed to focus on what he was there to do—but damn, she made him horny.

The two men sat there staring at each other. Neither one said a word, not wanting to be the first to speak. Each one was trying to intimidate the other. After about a minute, Chief Hill finally broke the silence.

"Well, I take it Scar won't be joining us."

"That's right," Sticks said, still without emotion on his face or in his voice.

"That's too bad," the chief responded.

Each man was being very careful not to give anything away in this little game of cat and mouse that they were playing with each other.

The chief continued, "You said you wanted to talk. So?"

"You wearing a wire?" Sticks asked. He wasn't about to say anything until he knew for sure.

"No. Are you?" the chief shot back without hesitation.

"How I know you ain't lying?" Sticks was being very cautious.

"You could pat me down, but that isn't going to help. I could have planted mic's in the diner. So, I guess you'll just have to trust me," the chief said with a smirk on his face.

"How about we each ask an incriminating question and we both answer truthfully," Sticks responded with his own smirk.

The chief chuckled. "Okay." He had a look of amusement on his face, but he was thinking he may have underestimated Sticks. Maybe Sticks was smarter than he was giving him credit for. He would have to proceed with caution.

"You first." The chief sat with his hands folded on top of the table.

Sticks started right away. "Were you going to kill Tiphani Fuller when she escaped from the back of your car?"

"Yes," the chief answered immediately. "Were you involved in the ambush of the SWAT team that resulted in the death of Detective Rodriguez?"

"Hell yes." Sticks' whole face lit up with a huge smile.

The chief got pissed at how pleased Sticks was to answer that question. Now he just wanted to get this over with before he lost his cool.

"Satisfied? Can you finally tell me why we are here?" Chief Hill asked to move things along.

"Scar needs to know when and where the roadblocks are in Baltimore."

"I can't tell him that."

"He says he will make it worth your while."

"I can't do it," Chief Hill said, shaking his head.

Sticks wasn't surprised by the chief's resistance. Scar had told him that Chief Hill would probably try to get more money out of the deal by saying no at first.

"He said he has paid you a lot of money over the years. For this information, he will triple what he normally pays you." Sticks said what Scar had coached him to say.

"So, Scar is still in Baltimore?"

"I didn't say that."

Sticks answered so quickly that the chief could safely assume that Scar was still in Baltimore. The chief sensed now was his opportunity to try to get Scar out of hiding.

"I need to speak with Scar in person if this is going to happen."

"You speakin' with me now. I got the cash in my trunk. Scar says, you do this, this is the last thing he'll ask you to do. You never have to work for him again."

This angered the chief, that Scar thought he could dictate when and how he could end their relationship. Chief Hill knew working for Scar was wrong, but he always felt that it was his choice, not Scar's.

"Well, you tell Scar, if he wants to get out of Baltimore, he needs to speak with me in person. He doesn't decide when I stop working for him; I do."

"He ain't gonna like hearing that. You should just take the cash, son. Simple and easy, then you out."

"If we don't meet, he can expect the roadblocks to be doubled and the manhunt to intensify even more." The chief was pissed.

"You makin' a mistake," Sticks said matter-of-factly.

"I don't think so."

Chief Hill got up and walked out the door. He was hoping that his aggressive tactic was going to work. He thought about following Sticks, because he was almost certain Sticks would be going directly back to Scar, but when he got to his car, he looked back at the diner and saw Sticks watching him from the front door. He would just have to wait and see how Scar would react. Chief Hill started his car and drove away from the diner.

After the chief was out of sight, Sticks walked over to Flex, who was still sitting in the Nissan Maxima. As Sticks approached the car, Flex stepped out of the backseat to greet him.

"What's good?" Flex asked as they greeted each other with a pound.

"Walk with me," Sticks said as he started toward his Escalade. He didn't say anything to Flex as they walked.

After the chief took off, being the opportunist that he was, Sticks had hatched a plan. Now he was consumed with what he would tell Scar and how he could use all of what just happened to his advantage. He needed to come up with a story that would keep Scar off his back.

When he got to his Escalade, he pushed the button on the remote to open the trunk.

"You done good today," he said as he leaned into the trunk and opened the briefcase that was sitting there. This was the bribe money that was intended to go to Chief Hill.

"Oh shit! That's some serious paper." Flex had never seen so much cash.

Sticks took about a quarter of the money and handed it to Flex. "There's plenty more where this came from. You know Scar ain't never be givin' you loot like this. Remember who this come from. Someday you might have to declare who your loyalty lies with."

"Yo, good lookin', B! You ever need anything, I'm yo' man! I'm the loyalest nigga out there." Flex couldn't hide his excitement.

That's exactly what Sticks wanted to hear. The almighty dollar worked its magic on Flex. Sticks now had him where he wanted. A few more payouts like this and he would be following Sticks and not Scar.

"You earned it, nigga. Just don't be flauntin' this shit in front of the other young bucks. This is coming from my own stash, and I don't want every nigga tryin' to do me favors so they can get a piece of my cash. You feel me?" Sticks lied, trying to make sure that Scar would never find out that he took the money for himself.

Flex assured Sticks, "You ain't gotta worry. I don't want none of them tryin' to get their paws on my shit neither."

"I hear you. I'm out." Sticks laughed as he closed the briefcase and then the trunk.

Sticks needed to take the rest of the money and stash it before he went back to Scar. He also needed a little bit of time to get the story straight in his head. It had to sound legit when he told Scar that Chief Hill took the money.

***

"The fuck you mean, he stole the money?" Scar clenched his jaw.

"He up and took that shit. He told me he ain't helpin' us, then he stuck his mu'fuckin' pistol in my face."

"Why the fuck you ain't fight him back?"

"I would have, but he took me by surprise. I turned my back for a second, and when I turned back around, he was pointing that shit in my face."

"Why you ain't hit the gun out his hand?"

"I couldn't. He was just outta my reach. I tried, but he just stepped back." Sticks demonstrated the movement.

"Nigga, you need to fight fire with fire. Pull yo' shit out and blast that fool." Scar was becoming so tense that his body was starting to ache.

"That's the fucked up thing. I wasn't strapped. I left my piece at my crib." Sticks couldn't tell if his lie was working.

"So, you just let this nigga walk with my cash?" Scar's breathing was starting to sound like a thoroughbred after the Kentucky Derby.

"Hell no! I chased after this mu'fucka. As soon as this nigga took off, I ran to my car and followed. We was speeding all over the road like *The Fast and the Furious* until he drove right into a roadblock. He sailed right through that shit, probably flashed his badge then laughed like a mu'fucka. I had to stop chasing him and go the back roads. You know they be lookin' for me too. I wouldn't be no good to you if I'm locked up. "

Scar went ballistic. The remote control flew across the room, slammed into the wall, and smashed into a million pieces. He shattered the glass coffee table by stomping on it, and he kicked in his beloved sixty-inch flat screen.

"I want this mu'fucka dead! He took my money; I'ma take his life!" Scar wolfed as his crew tried to avoid all the debris flying about the room. "Gimme yo' gat. I'ma do this nigga myself!" Scar barked at one of his young crew members. "No one steals from Scar Johnson!"

The young crew member handed Scar his 9 mm. Scar was pacing back and forth, practically foaming at the mouth, he was so heated. He was like a caged, rabid pit bull.

In all of his years in the Dirty Money Crew, Sticks had rarely seen Scar this mad. None of the young crew members in the house had ever seen him like this. They had no idea what to do, except just stand there and hope they didn't become a target of Scar's wrath.

"Y'all get the fuck out!" Sticks ordered to the other crew members.

They didn't waste any time scurrying out of the room. They looked like a bunch of cockroaches running back behind the walls when the lights get turned on. Sticks remained in the room, waiting for Scar to calm down a little. When it seemed as though Scar was ready to listen, Sticks began trying to talk some sense into him.

"Scar, we need to think about this," Sticks said calmly. He didn't want Scar having any contact with Chief Hill and finding out who really stole the money.

Hearing Sticks, Scar knew he was right. They did need to think about this. He needed to keep a low profile, and going after the chief of police would bring too much heat. His pacing started slowing down, but his mind was still moving a mile a minute, trying to figure out what they should do.

When Scar's pacing stopped altogether, in a calmer, more rational tone, he spoke. "You right. This mu'fucka did the one thing he thought would piss me off so much that I would come after him. He knew I wouldn't just come and talk to him face to face. I'm too smart for that. So, he stole my money to try and get me out. We lost him. He ain't with us no more."

"Exactly," Sticks reassured.

"He almost got me. Damn." Scar was sort of impressed that the chief was that smart. He was more impressed with himself that he figured it out and saw the chief's plan.

"What you want me to do?" Sticks asked.

"Nothin'. You good for now. Since we ain't got the chief, we gon' have to put the heat on my brother Derek now. A little birdie told me he gettin' out tomorrow." Scar was going to reinforce to Derek that he had his kids and it would be in his best interests to help him escape the city.

"I can do that."

"Nah. I want him to see some new faces. Show that nigga we an ever-expanding unit. I'ma get Day on that," Scar said. "Hand me yo' phone."

Sticks reluctantly did as he was asked. He couldn't understand why Scar wouldn't just let him handle everything. He was getting fed up and didn't know how much longer he could stand being disrespected by Scar.

Scar took the phone and dialed Day's number. "Yo. Where you at?" he asked when Day answered.

"I'm up north," Day lied. He was still in the city.

"Get your ass down here."

"It's gonna take me a minute. Tryin' to work some shit up here." Day easily lied again.

"Fuck that! I'm tellin' you to get back here," Scar snapped.

"A'ight, I'm on my way. Be there in a few hours."

"Nah, you know what? Just go straight to County and pick up Derek Fuller. He gettin' sprung tomorrow."

"I'll be waiting for him."

"I'ma text you two pictures later—one of Derek, and one to show him. When you get it, call me so I can tell you what to say to this nigga," Scar instructed.

"Bet," Day said and ended the conversation.

Scar tossed the phone back to Sticks, sat on the couch, and started rolling a blunt. He was on edge and needed to chill out. With the manhunt for himself and Tiphani still going strong, he felt like Bin Laden hiding out in a cave in Pakistan. He needed to get the fuck out of that house and Baltimore soon or he was going to go crazy.

He took a hit from the blunt then said, "I'ma kill this mu'fuckin' Chief Hill," as smoke came pouring out of his mouth like smoke from a fog machine.

Chapter 7

The Kids Are All Right . . . For Now

Day sat outside of the Baltimore County Jail, looking up at the gray sky and thinking about Halleigh. He was really starting to feel her, and he couldn't stop thinking about her bangin' body. The more he pictured her firm breasts and perfectly round ass, the more he got turned on. It was starting to make him horny as shit. He wanted to bust a nut so bad, he actually thought for a second that he should take a chance of leaving the jail to go fuck one of the Dirty Money Crew's hoes real quick.

Get your head on, nigga. She's way off limits. You're here to do a job, he thought as he snapped out of his daydream.

To try to occupy his mind with thoughts other than Halleigh, Day reached over and turned the car radio to his favorite station, 92Q. He took out his cell phone and looked at the picture Scar had texted earlier of his niece and nephew sitting on his lap. It was like a family portrait where everyone has huge smiles on their faces—except for the fact that Scar was holding a gun and pointing it at the camera, and the kids had looks of terror on their faces. This didn't really help Day get his mind off of Halleigh. When he looked at Scar's nephew, it reminded him of Malek Jr., which, of course, made him think of Halleigh.

He was just about to drive away from the jail when he saw the gates start to open. Thinking it might be Derek, he waited. Sure enough, when the gates fully opened, Detective Derek Fuller came walking out. He walked to the edge of the curb, stopped, and looked around.

Derek stared as a black Cadillac Escalade slowly came toward him and stopped with the passenger side door directly in front of him. He couldn't see inside because of the tint on the windows, but he thought it might be someone the mayor had sent. Just before he reached for the door handle, the passenger's window slowly came down. When he saw the person sitting behind the wheel, he knew it wasn't someone from the mayor's office. Someone from the mayor's office would have been wearing a suit. This guy was wearing a purple-and-black leather Baltimore Ravens jacket with a white tank top underneath.

"Scar sent me. Get in." Day leaned on the passenger's seat so he could see out the window and into Derek's eyes.

"I can take the bus." Derek started walking away.

Keeping pace, Day drove next to him so he could keep talking. "You're going to want to hear what I have to say."

"I doubt that."

"You want to see your kids?" Day showed Derek the picture of his kids with Scar.

This stopped Derek in his tracks and he leaned in the window. "You son of a bitch! Where are my kids? Where the fuck are my kids! They better not have one hair on their heads harmed or I will kill you!"

Day just sat there silently, watching Derek lose his mind. He let him keep screaming until he was finished, then calmly said with a slight smirk on his face, "Don't worry. Your kids are fine. Now, if you will get in and listen, you will be that much closer to seeing them again."

Derek was glaring at Day with hate in his eyes. If he had a gun, he would have shot him right there. Little did he know that Day wanted to shoot him just as much. Day would never forget that Derek was the one who shot and killed his mentor, Malek. If Day didn't need Derek's help, he would have shot him the second he saw him.

After a few seconds staring Day down, Derek got in the SUV and they drove away from the jail. Day hopped on I-83 and headed north.

"Where are we going?" Derek asked impatiently.

Day ignored him and just kept driving. He wanted to fuck with Derek and knew this would piss him off. Since he couldn't shoot him, he figured he could at least have some fun. Making Derek angry and uncomfortable was going to be entertaining for Day.

"I asked you a fucking question." Derek was losing his patience.

"You hungry? I know you ain't had any decent food in a while." Day was still fucking with Derek.

"Cut the bullshit! Where the fuck are we going?" Derek yelled. When it came to his kids, his fuse was very short.

"You better chill the fuck out, nigga. You in no position to be gettin' an attitude." Day said, reminding Derek who was in charge.

Derek got it. He wasn't about to jeopardize his kids. He remained silent. He couldn't believe that his brother was threatening the life of his kids. How had their relationship gotten so bad? He remembered back to how happy he was when he found his brother after being separated all those years. Their lives had gone in totally opposite directions after they left the foster home, but that didn't matter. When they reunited, their bond was just as tight as when they were kids—until Scar broke that bond by fucking Derek's wife. Now their brotherly bond was shattered beyond repair.

They drove a little farther without speaking and Day pulled into the Mondawmin Mall parking lot. Since it was a weekday afternoon, there weren't many cars in the lot. Day drove to a particularly deserted section and parked his SUV far away from any other vehicle. He sat there for about a full minute, not saying a word. This was killing Derek. He wanted to scream and punch this dude in his face, but if he did, it would jeopardize his children, and Derek was going to do everything in his power to make sure those two beautiful children remained safe. So, he sat there biting his tongue.

"Scar needs your help," Day began.

"When can I see my kids?"

"After you help Scar."

"I want to see my kids and I want to see Scar," Derek demanded.

Day ignored the request and continued with what Scar wanted him to say. He wasn't about to go into detail about why he couldn't see Scar or his kids.

"Scar needs you to get the mayor to pull some strings and get him out of Baltimore."

"I suppose he wants to escape with his whore Tiphani, too. Tell Scar I'm not doing shit until I see my kids and I meet with him," Derek said coldly.

"Tiphani's on her own. She disappeared into thin air. He wants that bitch dead," Day corrected Derek.

This surprised Derek. He thought for sure that they would be together considering the way Tiphani fell for Scar and how addicted she seemed to his dick. She was always clingy, and Derek knew that Tiphani needed that dick constantly. Unless, of course, this dude was lying. There was no way to tell for sure, so Derek figured he just needed to assume it was true.

"I can find her. I promise. Just let me have my kids back," Derek pleaded.

"If you do as Scar says, you'll have your kids."

"Fuck him," Derek said more to himself than to Day.

Day didn't say anything. He waited for an answer from Derek. Derek was staring out the window, watching a mother and her two children walk across the empty parking lot and into the mall. His heart was aching for his children. He needed to figure out a way to get them back. He was between a rock and a hard place.

"Just do it. Time's running out." Day took out his phone and showed Derek the picture one more time.

Derek started to tear up when he saw his kids. They were tears of sadness and anger. Seeing their faces made him sad, but seeing that Scar had guns around them infuriated him.

"You tell my brother Stephon that I will do what he wants. Then I'm coming for him and Tiphani, and I will kill them both." Derek was seething with anger.

He had no intention of really helping Scar. He only said it to protect his children. He figured if he could string Scar along, it would buy him some time to find out where he was hiding, and buy his kids more time to live. His children were the only thing in this life he cared for anymore. He was prepared to kill anyone who came in between him and his children, and he would start with Scar and that cheating, conniving bitch Tiphani.

Day handed Derek a throwaway cell phone. "Keep this on you. I'll call when we need to meet again. You better have made some moves when I come callin'."

Derek stepped out of the SUV determined to save his children and annihilate his brother. Stephon "Scar" Johnson was going to regret the day he betrayed his brother.

Chapter 8

A Picture is Worth a Thousand Words

The waiting room to Mayor Steele's office was silent except for the steady clicking of his secretary's keyboard. Susan was diligently typing up the mayor's next speech. Derek sat on a leather chair against the wall, watching her. Susan had stopped him from going directly into the office, telling Derek that the mayor was on a very important phone call. Derek had been waiting for fifteen minutes, and he was getting impatient. He just wanted to get this meeting over with so he could get on with saving his children.

"Hello, Susan. You are looking lovely as usual." The mayor's chief of staff, Dexter Coram, walked into the room.

"Hi, Dexter." Susan glanced up at Dexter and went right back to typing.

"When are you going to finally have dinner with me?" He was leaning over with his hands flat on the desk.

Without looking up from the computer screen, Susan answered, "Never."

Susan didn't understand why Dexter insisted on always asking her to dinner. It was obvious to her that Dexter was one of those down low brothers. He acted as if he liked women, but she had seen him flirt with guys enough times to know that behind closed doors, Dexter liked to get nasty with other dudes.

"One of these days you'll say yes." Dexter winked at her, but Susan ignored him.

"The mayor's busy," she told him. "You'll have to wait."

Dexter shrugged. As he turned away from Susan's desk to go sit down, he noticed Derek sitting there.

"Is that who I think it is? Mmmm . . ." he whispered to Susan with his eyebrows raised.

Susan just rolled her eyes and kept typing. To her, Dexter was the epitome of sleaze.

Dexter kept staring at Derek as he went and stood directly in front of him with his hand reached out. "Hi. I'm Dexter Coram."

"Derek." He shook Dexter's hand.

"I like that name." Dexter was smiling and wouldn't let go of Derek's hand.

"Thanks." Derek ripped his hand from Dexter's.

"My friends call me Dee." Dexter stayed standing in front of Derek.

"Good for you." Derek looked to Susan.

Dexter went to sit in the leather chair directly across from Derek. He was looking at Derek like he was waiting for him to say something.

"Get it?" Dexter asked.

Derek really didn't feel like having a conversation with this freak, so he just kept staring at the wall and didn't respond.

"Dee Coram. It sounds like the word *decorum*." Dexter had a little grin on his face, getting a kick out of his own corny joke. It was a lie anyway; no one ever called him Dee.

There was still no response from Derek, who just wanted this guy to shut up.

"Yeah, I don't think it's that funny either," Dexter said, sounding disappointed.

Susan continued to type while listening to this sad attempt at flirting by Dexter. She was grossed out by the chief of staff, and when he did this kind of stuff, it made her dislike him even more. She had never been around someone so weasely, smarmy, and sleazy. Nothing would make her happier than to never have to speak to him or see him again.

After a few minutes of silence, Dexter couldn't help himself. He had to say something to Derek.

"You were in jail, right?" he asked, staring seductively at Derek.

Derek was losing his patience. He just wanted to be left alone until it was time to go in to see the mayor. Derek ignored the comment again, but the dude wouldn't stop.

"Must have been scary with all of those guys in there." Dexter paused for a response and again got nothing. "I can tell you worked out while you were locked up."

This shit was getting out of control, and Derek was at his breaking point. Dexter's compliment was an obvious lie. Derek had lost weight, and his body was nowhere near as ripped as it used to be. He spent most of his time in the infirmary trying to recover from his stab wounds.

"You have nice shoulder definition. I like it. How do you get that? I work out, but I can't get my shoulders as nice as yours. The ladies must love you." Dexter couldn't stop himself. "What do you think, Susan?"

Derek let out a small moan and shook his head in disgust. His face was starting to tighten up with anger. He looked over at Susan, who had a look of disgust on her face too.

When she made eye contact with Derek, she shrugged her shoulders as a sign of camaraderie. She could tell that Derek was just as irritated by Dexter as she was. She

wanted to say something to Dexter, but he was her su-
perior and she would risk being fired if she did. So, she
said nothing, figuring that one day Dexter would get his.

When Derek wouldn't answer him, Dexter finally
took the hint and stopped talking. That didn't stop
him from staring, though. He was trying desperately to
make eye contact with Derek. He was checking him out
from head to toe. As he was sitting there, he discreetly
reached into the inside pocket of his suit jacket and
pulled out his BlackBerry. He surreptitiously started
taking pictures of Derek's crotch while pretending to
check e-mails.

Susan had seen Dexter do this before and realized
right away what was happening. She started clearing
her throat in order to get Derek's attention. He was too
busy trying to ignore Dexter, so he wasn't picking up
on her signals. Seeing he wasn't catching on, she continued a little louder. Derek still didn't look her way.
She started coughing, and that finally caused Derek to
look at her. With her eyes, she signaled toward Dexter,
while making a motion with her hands like she was
pushing the shutter button on a camera.

Dexter was so consumed with his picture taking that
he had no clue of anything going on around him. He
was in his own perverted world.

Derek didn't really understand what Susan was trying to say, but when he looked over at Dexter, he realized right away what this freak was doing. That was
definitely the final straw. Derek leaped from his chair
and lunged at Dexter.

"What the fuck you doing, nigga?"

Derek didn't want to cause any trouble in the mayor's
office, so he'd tried ignoring Dexter, but a dude taking a
picture of his dick was cause for a beat down. Derek tried
grabbing the BlackBerry from Dexter, but he wouldn't

give it up. He held on with all of his strength. He wasn't about to let Derek see what was on there. They struggled back and forth, each trying to gain control of the phone.

"Cut it out!" Dexter squealed like a girl.

"Give me the phone, motherfucker!"

Finally, Derek let go of the phone with one hand, cocked it, and punched the shit out of Dexter's face. Dexter let out a high-pitched scream and let go of the phone. While he was hunched over trying to protect his face from any more of Derek's punches, Derek took the phone and hurled it against the wall as hard as he could. As the phone smashed against the wall and Derek turned to beat on Dexter, the mayor's office door swung open wildly.

"What's going on out here?" Mayor Steele yelled.

Susan was a little disappointed to see the mayor come out of his office and interrupt the beating. She had been watching the whole episode with delight. Dexter was getting his comeuppance sooner than she expected, and she was hoping he was about to get more. When Derek punched Dexter, she thought, *Karma's a bitch, you sleazeball.*

"This freak is taking pictures of me on his cell phone."

"I am doing no such thing. This man attacked me for no reason."

"I should kick your ass for lying." Derek stepped toward Dexter with his fist cocked.

"Hey hey hey! Stop it! Both of you in my office, now!" the mayor bellowed.

"I'm not going in there with this fruitcake," Derek said.

"Ugh." Dexter rolled his eyes and pursed his lips.

"Either he comes in here, or no one comes in here. Take it or leave it." The mayor turned and walked into his office.

Derek looked at Dexter, who was sitting there with a smug look on his face; then he looked at Susan, who had a sympathetic look on hers. He decided he should just get the meeting over with. *Fuck it,* he thought and walked into the mayor's office as Dexter followed.

Susan watched the door to the mayor's office close then went back to typing, this time with a little grin on her face.

The mayor stood behind his desk and watched the two men enter his office. He was not happy with either of them.

"Sit down, both of you." He waited for the two men to sit before he continued. "I don't know and I don't care what just happened out there, but you two are going to have to learn to work together."

"Why is he even in here?" Derek asked.

"After today, you and I will no longer have any contact. Dexter will be representing me. Anything you and I have to say to one another will go through Dexter," Mayor Steele said.

"How do I know I can trust this sneaky, down low creep?" Derek protested.

Dexter didn't say a word. During the exchange between the mayor and Derek, he had made his way to a mirror on the wall and was tending to the bruise forming on his face.

"Again, take it or leave it," Mayor Steele told Derek.

Derek didn't like it, but he had no choice. He needed the mayor on his side and whatever help the mayor could give. His children were his only concern at this point. He would do anything to get them back. If it meant having to deal with a punk like Dexter, then so be it. He would do it.

"Fine."

"Good," Mayor Steele said.

"I look forward to our time together." Dexter cocked his head slightly and grinned as he looked at Derek's reflection in the mirror. Dexter could swear that he was watching the bruise swell up on the spot. He was concerned about how it was going to affect his looks. All he wanted to do was get some ice and try to stop the swelling.

It took everything in Derek's power to not stand up and kick that grin off of Dexter's face. Instead, he just clenched his jaw and said nothing.

The mayor chose to ignore the blatant taunt as well. He had seen Dexter do his thing before, but didn't feel like dealing with it. Even if he was a bit of a kiss-ass at times and sort of creepy, Dexter was loyal to the mayor, and right now, the mayor needed as many people on his side as possible.

"As we discussed, I got you out of prison, so now it's time for you to do me a favor." The mayor leaned back and folded his hands in front of his chest.

"How much does he know?" Derek said, referring to Dexter.

"Everything. Feel free to talk," the mayor said.

Derek was still skeptical of Dexter and didn't feel comfortable saying what he wanted to say. "Everything?" he asked.

"Ugh. Yes, I know everything. I'm the chief of staff. I know the deal you two have, so just say whatever it is you want to say." Dexter was still facing the mirror as he spoke. He would have turned around, but he wanted Derek to see his booty. He thought it was his best asset.

Derek was so frustrated by Dexter and his tone that he just blurted out what he had to say. "Fine. Before I can help you kill Tiphani, I need help killing Scar."

"Oh please. Just because he fucked your wife doesn't mean we should help you kill him," Dexter announced, still checking himself out in the mirror. He thought the bruise made him look tough. Maybe Derek would think it looked sexy and become attracted to him.

Derek was seriously on the verge of giving this freak a beat down that would put him in the intensive care unit. "Shut the fuck up. I'm in a meeting with the mayor. After today I will speak to you, but right now, you don't exist in my world." Derek faced the mayor. "Look, I can get Tiphani. I just need my kids to get her to show her face. Scar is holding my kids hostage, and he isn't going to give them up easy."

"Do you think Scar is still in Baltimore?" Mayor Steele was interested.

"I know he is. He sent one of his men to pick me up from jail. He thinks I'm going to help him get out of Baltimore. I told him I would speak to you about it. If he's watching me, he probably thinks that's why I'm here."

"What does he want me to do?" the mayor asked.

"He wants to know about the roadblocks."

"Dexter, double the roadblocks in the city," the mayor directed.

"Yes, sir." Dexter was still surveying his face in the mirror, though his mood was improving. He wore makeup at home all the time, but had been too afraid to wear it to work. Now he could use the bruises as an excuse to wear makeup in the office for a week or two.

"So, what can we do? We have no idea where he is. We've been looking for this son of a bitch everywhere," the mayor continued.

"I'll find him, and when I do, I'll take him out. I just need access to the police department files and a few men to help." Derek waited for an answer.

The mayor wasn't going to give an answer right away. Derek's offer sounded good, but he wanted to think it over. He spun around in his chair and looked out the window onto the streets of Baltimore. The people had no trust in him and no respect for his police force. He was losing his city, and he blamed it all on Scar Johnson. He needed to do something to take back control of the city.

"Okay. I'll have Chief Hill get in contact with you. He can help you with whatever you need." Mayor Steele stood up.

"Thank you." Derek stood up as well and shook the mayor's hand.

"Good luck. This city needs to be rid of scum like Scar and Tiphani."

Derek nodded in agreement. He turned and headed out the door, happy to have gotten what he wanted out of the meeting. Now it was time to find his kids.

As soon as Derek was out of the room, Mayor Steele picked up the phone and dialed Chief Hill.

"Hello," Chief Hill answered.

"It's Mathias. Derek Fuller was just here. I told him you would assist him in finding Scar Johnson."

"How? I don't know where he is."

"I know that. Just help with whatever you can. What I really need you to do is follow him. When he finds Scar, you need to make sure he doesn't kill him. We need Scar alive. I believe I don't have to tell you what needs to be done to Detective Fuller when he finds Scar." Without waiting for an answer, the mayor hung up the phone.

"Sneaky, sir. I like it. Use Derek to find Scar, then kill Derek and capture Scar. The city will see that you are still in control. Perhaps even better is if it could look like Scar fought back and was killed while being apprehended?" Dexter smiled at the mayor.

"Perhaps." The mayor turned to look out the window again, watching Derek walk across the plaza to his car. He hoped Derek could find Scar fast so this entire ordeal could be over. As he watched Derek drive off, he thought, *I hope this is the last time I see you alive, Detective Fuller.*

Chapter 9

Death of a Family

Halleigh's three-bedroom house sat at the end of a cul de sac in a suburb of Baltimore. She moved in because she liked the fact that there was only one way into the neighborhood. It was ideal; she would never be trapped. If anyone ever came for her, she would see them coming and could make her escape out the back and into the woods behind the house.

She loved this house. She loved that she could let Malek Jr. run around outside and not worry about him. There were no gangbangers trying to recruit her child, no hustlers on the street corners, and no shootouts. The only drive-bys were done by the mailman when he came to put mail in her mailbox. It was the complete opposite of what she grew up in, and she loved that she could let her son grow up in such a wonderfully calm environment.

On the outside, she seemed relaxed and blissful, but Halleigh had a dark secret that wouldn't go away. To her neighbors and everyone in town she seemed happy, but she wouldn't be completely at ease until she knew that Scar Johnson and Derek Fuller were dead. It was the one thing that was driving her. She couldn't be truly happy until she had exacted revenge on the two men responsible for the death of her man.

Halleigh relaxed a little when she looked out the front window and saw Dayvid's SUV pulling into the driveway. It calmed her nerves, and she felt relief whenever she saw his Escalade.

Dayvid and Halleigh had been after Scar and Derek since the day Malek was gunned down. They had secretly been following Scar and his crew from a distance, making sure that no one ever saw them. Recently Dayvid took the most risk by revealing himself and infiltrating Scar's Dirty Money Crew. This caused Halleigh to worry every day that he would be found out. Not only would her chance at revenge die, but so would Dayvid. Recently Halleigh was realizing that she had feelings for Dayvid that went beyond friendship and to lose him would devastate her. She felt they had been taking chances and tempting fate long enough. They had followed both men and plotted their deaths; now it was time to put an end to both men.

"M.J., Dayvid is here," Halleigh called out to her son, who came running.

When Dayvid opened the door, M.J. jumped right into his arms and hugged him tight. It was obvious to Halleigh that Malek Jr. loved Dayvid. He had told Halleigh a few days earlier that he wished Dayvid lived with them. This made her think that it wouldn't be a bad idea to have Dayvid move in. She had plenty of space. He could have his own room, and it would give M.J. a male figure in the house. Still, she was torn between wanting to honor Malek and wanting to explore her new feelings for Dayvid. Having him around more would give Halleigh a chance to see if she really wanted more of a relationship with Dayvid.

"Hey, little man." Dayvid tossed Malek Jr. in the air and caught him.

"Play in room!" Malek Jr. announced happily.

Dayvid looked to Halleigh to make sure it would be all right.

"You can play for fifteen minutes, and then it's time to eat dinner." Halleigh tapped Malek Jr. on his butt.

Wasting no time, Malek Jr. jumped down from Dayvid's arms and ran to his room with a big smile on his face.

"He's a trip." Dayvid laughed and followed M.J. to his room.

For the next fifteen minutes, Malek Jr. was a whirlwind of energy. He tried to play with every toy he had in his room, finally settling on playing a game of pretend football. He had Dayvid be the quarterback, and he was the wide receiver/running back. They would pretend to score touchdowns and celebrate. Then they would pretend to stand on the sidelines and watch as their defense played. Malek Jr. was in heaven.

Halleigh heard the boys having so much fun that she gave them an extra fifteen minutes to play before she called out, "Okay. Dinner is ready."

The boys came running into the kitchen. Malek Jr. was wearing his Ravens jersey and a football helmet way too big for his tiny head.

"Mama, we win football." He held his arms up in victory.

"That's great. Now sit down and eat." She smiled.

For the next forty-five minutes they ate dinner. They talked, they told jokes and laughed. Everyone was having a great time. It was like they were a real family getting together at the end of a day. Halleigh felt comfortable and happy.

"Time for bed, little man," Dayvid said when dinner was over.

"You put bed?" Malek Jr. asked.

"Sure. If it's okay with your mom." He looked to Halleigh.

Halleigh smiled and gave him a nod of approval.

After reading to him and waiting for him to fall asleep, Dayvid came back out to the kitchen, where Halleigh was sitting. She was facing away from Dayvid, in her own world.

"What's on your mind?" Dayvid asked.

"He really loves you." She kept her back to Dayvid.

"I love him."

"That scares me. What happens if one day you never show up again?" She turned to him. After the night they just had, she wanted to walk right up and kiss him—the way a wife would kiss her husband, with passion and abandon.

"That won't happen. I'm making sure of that." Dayvid was having the same thought as Halleigh.

"How? There's no guarantee that you won't be killed. Scar could find out about us, and that would be the end of you. I don't want M.J. to have to go through that. He was too young to remember his dad getting shot, but he would be devastated to lose you." Halleigh was talking about her son's feelings for Dayvid, but she was also feeling the same way. She was not only concerned for how it would affect M.J. if Dayvid disappeared, but how it would affect her. She didn't want to admit it, but she was starting to fall in love.

"He won't find out. I promise. I'm one of his majors. He had me pick Detective Fuller up from jail and give him a warning."

"What?" Halleigh's tone instantly changed.

"I picked up Detective Fuller from jail and delivered a warning from Scar."

"Why the fuck didn't you shoot him on the spot?" Halleigh went from concerned to pissed in a split second.

"I couldn't. I'm working on something, and I have to play along with Scar for a little while longer."

"I'm getting sick of this waiting shit. You have the opportunity every day to kill Scar, but you don't do it. Now you have Detective Fuller, the man who shot Malek, in front of you, and you don't kill him. You need to man up and shoot these niggas." Halleigh was standing toe to toe with Dayvid.

"Chill. I have a plan."

"What plan? To be a pussy and don't kill these two motherfuckers?" Halleigh was letting the street come out of her. She wanted this whole thing to be over. She felt the sooner Scar and Fuller died, the sooner she could be sure that Dayvid and her son would be safe.

"Come on, Hal. Listen. I'm trying to set up a little piece of the business for us. I've been taking money from Scar, and he thinks his business is falling off. It's perfect timing. If I get blamed for Scar's death now, then we won't have anything set up for the future. I'm doing it for you and M.J. We just have to be patient."

"I'm done being patient. You tell me this all the time." She walked away from him.

"It's for us."

"What is this 'us' bullshit? There is no 'us.' It is me and my son. You are not part of that." Halleigh said the words that she hoped would hurt Dayvid and hopefully provoke him to finally kill Scar. Truthfully, she had wanted it to be "us" but was now getting confused about her true feelings.

Dayvid was hurt by that last comment. He wanted to be a part of Halleigh and M.J.'s lives forever. It was starting to feel to him that they were thinking the same thing. He was setting it up so that he could provide for them. His motivation used to be revenge, but now everything he did was motivated by how it would affect Halleigh and M.J. in the future.

"Fuck you, Halleigh. I'm trying to help you two." He glared at her.

"Well, fuck you too. We don't need your help, and if you ain't gonna kill them muthafuckas, then I will. Now, get out my house!" Halleigh had completely reverted back to her days on the street.

Dayvid was too shocked and hurt to say anything. He didn't want this argument to escalate into violence, so he just walked out of the house. The last thing he wanted to do was to leave. He was having an amazing night and didn't want it to end, but Halleigh was being disrespectful, and he couldn't stand there and take it. It didn't matter what he said; Halleigh wasn't going to listen. She was being unreasonable and wasn't appreciating what he was doing, so he was done trying to help. If she thought she could be on her own and handle her life, then let her try. He would continue setting up his little piece, but now it would all be for him and no one else. Halleigh was on her own.

Halleigh followed him to the door. "And don't come back!" She slammed the door closed. She stood with her back against the door for about a minute, until she couldn't hold her tears in any longer. She broke down and cried as she slid down to the floor.

She didn't want to kick Dayvid out, but she had let her emotions get the best of her. She was so confused. One minute she wanted to sleep with Dayvid, and the next she was fighting with him and kicking him to the curb. She sat there on the floor, feeling sorry for herself. She couldn't understand why her life continued to be a struggle. She just wanted it to be easy. She needed peace. She was sick of feeling pressure, sick of always looking over her shoulder thinking someone was after her. This evening had been so great with Dayvid and M.J., and it turned to shit in a matter of a few seconds.

Halleigh blamed Dayvid. He was holding off on killing Scar for no reason. Yeah, he said it was for them, but Halleigh didn't believe it. She had heard that same thing from Malek. He was always saying he would get out; he just had to do a little more so he could set up a future for her and their son. Look where that got him—killed. Why were the men in her life always saying it was for her? If he really wanted to do something for her, he would put an end to her struggle. He would kill Scar so she could get on with her life.

Halleigh allowed herself another minute or two for her pity party, and then she was done feeling sorry for herself. She wiped her face and picked herself up off the floor. If she wanted change in her life, she needed to be the one to make it. The only way Halleigh thought she could have peace of mind was if Scar and Derek Fuller were dead, so it was time for her to take matters into her own hands. If Dayvid couldn't do it, then she would.

Halleigh walked into her bedroom with a purpose. She went directly to her walk-in closet and started going through her clothes to find the most revealing and seductive clothes she had. *If you want something done right, you've got to do it yourself,* she thought as she rummaged through her wardrobe.

When she found the perfect outfit, she tried it on. Standing in front of the mirror and admiring her body, she said to herself, *Scar Johnson, your days are numbered, motherfucker.* She formed her hand into the shape of a gun, pointed it at the mirror, and mimed shooting someone. *Boom!*

Chapter 10

Dance of Death

It had been a few days since their fight, and Day had not seen or heard from Halleigh. He was depressed about it and couldn't stop replaying the fight over and over in his head. Even though he thought about going over there several times, his pride stopped him from doing so. She kicked him out. She was being unreasonable, so she needed to be the one to reach out to him. In the meantime, Day would continue to fuck with Scar's business and take as much money as he could. Then, when he had it all set, he would kill Scar and be set up for life—with or without Halleigh. He was trying to convince himself it would be better without her. It would be less of a headache. At the moment, he had a splitting one.

Day was sitting on the couch at Scar's place, trying to relieve the tension by rubbing his temples. He had been having stress headaches ever since the fight. He was having a hard time concentrating on anything. Not only was he stressed about Halleigh, but he was starting to second guess his strategy. Maybe Halleigh was right. Maybe he should just murk these two fools immediately. He was thinking that he might be acting too cautious, but how could infiltrating Scar's crew and basically working undercover be too cautious? He was taking a huge risk, not Halleigh. She helped out for a while, but now that he was in, she stayed out of the picture. Day was confused. He needed to sort this all out before he slipped up or his head exploded from the headaches.

The television was on, but Day had hardly been paying attention. He was supposed to be looking for any new information on Tiphani or the manhunt for Scar. It wasn't easy to get much from the television these days, as most news outlets had started to lose interest in the case. There were a few political scandals that they started focusing on. The mayor was eager to focus on them as well. It allowed him to pull focus from his poor handling of the Scar and Tiphani fiasco and point out the weaknesses of his political rivals.

Day tried to concentrate on the news, but his mind was obviously somewhere else. He had too many other things swirling around in his brain. Besides, he figured it was only a matter of time before Derek would come through with the information needed to get Scar out of Baltimore. That dude seemed desperate to get his kids back. Day didn't blame him, either. He would do the same thing for Malek Jr. Well, at least he would have, before Halleigh kicked him out.

Day watched as Chief Hill and Dexter Coram were answering some questions in front of City Hall. It was the usual political bullshit: say a lot of words without saying a goddamn thing that means anything.

Day was bored. His eyes were getting heavy, and he was about to fall asleep when Scar walked into the room. Day immediately woke up. Seeing Scar's face and his tense body language, Day sensed that Scar was not in a good mood.

"What the fuck they sayin'?" Scar tilted his head toward the television.

"Same old bullshit. A whole lot of nothin'." Day shrugged his shoulders.

Scar stood with his arms folded in front of him, watching the two men on the screen. His face was tight with anger. Day looked at him and saw him actually snarl when Chief Hill answered a question. Scar was more on edge today than he had been. He was oozing hate out of his pores.

After listening to them dance around questions, Scar was satisfied that they still had nothing on him. He quickly reached down for the remote and turned off the television.

"That fuck needs to be murked," Scar seethed.

"Who?"

"That thievin', muthafuckin' police chief," Scar said.

"You sayin' you want to kill the police chief?"

"The fuck did I just say? Yeah, I want to murk that mu'fucka."

"I thought he was on your payroll."

"You got a lotta fuckin'questions." Scar glared at Day.

"I'm just not sure if we need that kind of heat right now. Don't we already have enough comin' our way?" Day said.

"Nigga, I'm finished worrying about heat. I done killed cops before. I can kill cops again. A nigga steals from me, he needs to be murked." Scar swung his fist down like he was punching someone kneeling in front of him.

"Who stole from you?" Day got a little nervous when Scar mentioned someone stealing from him. Was Scar trying to say that he knew Day was stealing from him? Was he hinting to Day that he was going to kill him? Day immediately started trying to formulate a plan on how to fight his way out of the house.

"Chief Hill. Who the fuck you think we been talkin' about for the past five minutes?" Scar looked at Day like he was an idiot.

Day was relieved to know that Scar wasn't referring
to him, but he still needed to know the details. He had
to make sure not to make the same mistake and get
found out. The questions he had to ask would have to
be direct enough to get the answers he needed, but they
also couldn't be too specific. He didn't want to alert
Scar that he might be doing anything behind his back.
It was going to be a tightrope walk of questioning. One
false move could get him killed.

"For real? How you know that?"

"The nigga took a hun'ed-fifty Gs from me. Jacked
up Sticks and made off with the shit."

"Word? When?" Something didn't seem right to Day.
The only time that he knew Sticks and the chief coming
into contact was at the diner. That couldn't have been
when it happened, because Day had followed Sticks
there and seen everything that went down.

"The other day when Sticks went to talk to him." Scar
was visibly upset talking about it.

"At the diner?" Immediately Day regretted saying
this. He knew that Sticks and the chief were supposed
to meet, but there was no reason or way Day should
have known where. Day knew about the diner because
instead of going up north like he told Scar he was doing, he stayed in Baltimore and followed Sticks. He
had seen everything that went down, from when Sticks
approached Chief Hill in front of City Hall to the meeting that night at the diner. If Scar thought about it, he
would have realized that.

"Yep, the diner. Right in the parking lot. That cocky
mu'fucka." Scar's breathing was starting to quicken
and he began pacing. He was getting so agitated.

Day was in a bind. He knew Sticks' story was a lie,
but he couldn't tell that to Scar. He was supposed to
have been out of town when that went down. As angry

as Scar was at the moment, if he found out that Day lied to him, he was liable to kill him on the spot. How could he let Scar know this was a lie without giving himself away?

"Was anyone else there?" he asked.

"Nah."

This answer sparked a lot of questions in Day's head. *Why doesn't Scar know that Flex was in the parking lot? Does Flex know that Sticks said Chief Hill robbed him? Is Flex in on it?*

"I knew I should have gone as backup," Day said.

Day was trying to think of a way to make Scar figure out it was a lie. He thought back to that night for any clues. Halleigh had helped him with the surveillance that night. She was unknown to either Sticks or Chief Hill, so he figured she would be able to follow them on foot without fear of them recognizing her. He was correct. Halleigh had literally run right into Sticks. At first that made Day nervous, but then he watched as Sticks flirted with her, and he knew that she hadn't been recognized.

Day had Halleigh drive that night, and it was a good thing he did. After Halleigh went into the diner to try to hear their conversation, Day scanned the parking lot and saw Flex hiding out. Luckily he saw Flex before Flex saw him, so he was able to stay hidden.

When their meeting was over, Day watched as Chief Hill drove away. Then Sticks went into his car and handed Flex a stack of cash.

That's it! Day thought. When he saw it that night, he just assumed that Sticks was paying Flex for being his backup. That wasn't what it was, though. The money was either hush money from Sticks, or they were both in on it. The money in the trunk was probably Scar's money that was stolen—not by Chief Hill, but by Sticks.

Day had figured out who had the money. Now he just needed to find out how much Flex knew. He needed to find Flex and start asking some questions.

Day thought this was the best thing that could have happened. Day could convince Scar that Sticks was the reason the business was down. All of the money that Day had stolen from Scar could now be blamed on Sticks.

"I don't think you should take him out. Let's get a young buck to do it. Prove their loyalty," Day said.

Scar stopped pacing and looked at Day. He seemed to be searching Day's face for something. An answer? Day got a little uncomfortable as he sat there and Scar just stared at him. He couldn't tell what Scar was thinking. Maybe he'd pushed it too far and Scar was figuring out that he lied. Or was Scar starting to think that maybe Day was the one who stole the money? For the second time during this conversation, Day started to think of an escape plan. Day was on edge. He was trying to appear calm, but he didn't know if he was doing a good job at hiding his nervousness—which was making him even more nervous.

"You right. Who you think?" Scar finally broke the silence.

Day let out a sigh of relief, but quickly covered it up by fake coughing. He felt like he was starting to lose it. He had never been so unsure of himself around Scar before. He didn't know what was happening to him. One thing he knew was that he wasn't going to be able to keep feeling like this around Scar. If he did, he would eventually fuck up and end up dead. He was going to have to try to speed up his plan and take Scar out sooner than he thought.

"I like that youngin' Flex. He seem to have heart." Day composed himself and got back on track with his new plan. He could now have an excuse to meet with Flex alone.

"Yeah, I like that. He do seem to got heart," Scar said.

"A'ight, I can holla at him. You know where he at?"

"Nah. I got enough to be worryin' about than where some low level nigga be."

"I hear you. I'll find him." Day stood up to leave.

"Hold up. I need to holla at you for a minute." Scar stepped in front of Day.

This was it. Day was sure Scar was going to grill him about why the money was light. If he did, Day was prepared to put the blame on Sticks, but he would still try to keep his secret that he lied about being at the diner. Lying would be a disrespect to Scar, and in the Dirty Money Crew, that was cause for death.

"What's up?" Day stayed standing.

"Things been fucked up lately." Scar was again staring at Day.

"Word." Day was going to try to say as little as possible until he knew where Scar was going with this.

"Money been light." Scar was expressionless. "I think I know why."

Day prepared himself for what was coming next. Scar was going to bring the hammer down on him. Day's body tensed up, and his mind was going through a million different scenarios and lies all at once.

"Why?" Day balled his fists, ready to fight to the death.

Scar didn't answer right away. He stood about two feet in front of Day and just shook his head slowly from side to side, holding eye contact with Day the entire time. The silence was killing Day. He had two choices: strike first and take Scar off guard, or wait and see what Scar's move would be. Day always thought of himself as a man of action, so he was going to go out swinging. He started toward Scar.

"It's me," Scar said.

Day stopped himself before he took his first step.

"I've been unfocused about the product. This man-hunt and being holed up in this dump has made me lose focus."

Day didn't say a word. He was two steps away from punching Scar in his face and possibly putting an end to his own life. He was trying to wrap his mind around how lucky he had just gotten.

Scar continued, "I need to get out of here and get my mind straight. Go talk to Derek and see what he got for us. Once I'm out of B-More, I can get the money flowing in the right direction again." He walked over to his desk and sat down.

"A'ight, boss. I'll reach out to that nigga." Day sat down.

The door opened and Sticks entered the room. The smile on his face and the bounce in his step let them know that he was in a good mood. He was wearing his usual outfit of a fitted Baltimore Orioles baseball hat, tight T-shirt, baggy jeans, and Timberland boots.

"What up, fam?" Sticks walked to the middle of the room.

"The fuck you come barging in like the drug squad for?" Scar barked.

"I got something for you." Sticks had a big smile on his face.

"Wipe that corny smile off yo' face. The only reason you should be barging into my space is because you got a million dollars for me."

"It ain't a million dollars," Sticks said.

"Then get the fuck out. My man and me are having some serious conversations." Scar motioned over to Day.

Normally this would have really pissed Sticks off, but right now he had something that he knew would make Scar happy. After Scar saw what he had, he would forget about Day.

"It looks like a million dollars. Just wait and take a look. I guarantee you'll want to love it." Sticks was loving this. He turned and left the room.

Day looked at Scar and shrugged. They didn't have to wait long for Sticks to come back in with his surprise—a woman who was following behind him.

The moment she entered the room, Day's eyes widened. It was Halleigh. She was dressed in a short mini skirt that barely covered her ass, a see-through tank top, and stripper heels. She looked like she just got off the pole.

Halleigh saw Day immediately and stopped for just a split second, but she composed herself and got on with what she was there to do. She acted like she didn't know who the fuck Day was.

"I met this chick the other night. She bad, right?" Sticks grabbed her ass.

Day flinched and almost jumped out of his seat, but he restrained himself in time so that no one noticed.

Sticks continued, "I know you heated about losing that money, and you been stressed lately, so I figured I would bring her over for you. I haven't even touched her yet. I saved her to let you have first crack, and then we can run that train."

Halleigh stood there with a seductive look on her face, not saying a word. On the inside, her stomach was doing flips. She was nervous as shit, and to make matters worse, Day was there. She wanted to run over to him and tell him to leave, to say that she could handle it from here, but she couldn't let them know that she knew him.

Earlier in the day, Halleigh had followed Sticks into a bodega and acted like it was a coincidence. She walked up behind him while he was in the back pulling a forty-ounce of Colt 45 out of the cooler.

"Ain't I seen you at the diner the other night?" she said seductively.

"Oh shit, that's right. You the fine piece that gave me the wrong digits. What up with that?" Sticks said.

"I did? You must have gotten me so worked up that I wrote the wrong number. I'm here now, though." She rubbed his arm.

That was all she needed to do to get him. They flirted for a little while longer. She told him that she was a prostitute and she worked that diner sometimes for extra cash. She convinced him that she was looking for a pimp and that maybe he could be her pimp. When Sticks mentioned he worked with Scar, Halleigh said she would fuck both for free. Let them sample the goods before they put her to work. Sticks was all the way down with that. Now they were in the room with Scar.

"Damn, you a fine piece of ass. Come here. Let me see you closer." Scar stood up and made his way around his desk. Luckily for Halleigh, Malek never brought his business home, so Scar never knew about her.

Halleigh strutted over to him like a stripper walking over to collect her dollar bill from a john. Scar grabbed her breasts and stroked her arms. "Turn around. Let me see that ass," he instructed.

This was driving Day insane. He wanted to grab Halleigh and take her out of there. The sight of Scar touching her was making him crazy with jealousy and anger. He didn't know what to do. While Scar was putting his hands all over Halleigh, Sticks came and sat on the couch next to Day.

"I heard you got jacked by the chief," Day said to Sticks.

"Yeah, fuck him. Punk mu'fucka." Sticks was nonchalant with his answer, hoping the subject would be dropped. He continued watching Halleigh grind Scar.

In order to keep from flying into a rage, Day was going to try to get Sticks to fuck his story up about getting robbed. It would keep his mind occupied and maybe keep his eyes off of what was going on between Scar and Halleigh.

Day looked over at Halleigh as she walked to the center of the room.

"Put some music on. I want to dance for you." Halleigh slowly swayed her hips and pressed her breasts together.

Scar turned his stereo on and took a seat on the couch on the other side of Day. Sticks pulled out a blunt, lit it, and passed it to Scar. The three men watched as Halleigh began to seductively strip for them. It seemed to Day that every time they made eye contact, she would glare at him with hate in her eyes.

"This bitch is fine as fuck. I can't wait to get up inside that ass." Scar took a hit off his blunt.

Day continued his questioning of Sticks, hoping that Scar would listen and hear Sticks spew some bullshit.

"So, what happened? He held you up?" He looked at Sticks.

"Yeah, gun straight to my face."

"What kind of gun?"

"I don't fuckin' know. Stop askin' questions. I'm tryin' to watch this bitch dance for me." Sticks took the blunt back from Scar.

Halleigh had stripped down to just her lace thong. Scar and Sticks were getting worked up. She was doing splits and making her ass clap like a professional stripper. Day knew she had been forced into prostitution when she was younger, but now watching her dance, he thought maybe she had worked the pole at some point as well. He wanted to throw some clothes over her, pick her up, and run out of there.

Day was angry at everyone—at Sticks and Scar for putting their hands all over Halleigh's naked body, and at Halleigh for being there, dancing for them naked and allowing them to touch her. Day couldn't understand why Halleigh would be there doing this. She said she wanted Scar dead, but he didn't see how becoming one of Scar's hoes could accomplish that. Was this some sort of way to get back at Day because she was angry at him? Day started feeling like it was all his fault.

Halleigh was on her back in the middle of the room with her legs spread wide in a V shape. She closed them and spun around onto her stomach, arched her back, and got on all fours. She looked straight at Scar and licked her lips seductively.

"Come to daddy," he said.

Halleigh began slowly crawling toward Scar. Day was sick to his stomach, thinking that he was about to watch Halleigh suck Scar's dick. His whole body was taut with anger. He was desperate to try to stop it. Maybe he would kick her as she got close enough. Maybe he should just tell Scar that Sticks stole the money. He needed to figure out a way to break this thing up.

"Was anyone else in the parking lot when you got jacked?" Day asked Sticks.

"Shut up, nigga. This about to get real nasty up in here." Sticks wanted desperately to change the subject.

"Where was Flex?"

Sticks shot Day a sideways glance, thinking, *Why this nigga keep bringin' up this night? Does he know something he ain't sayin'?*

"The fuck should I know where that nigga be?" Sticks instantly got on guard. No one was supposed to know that Flex was there that night.

"It's just that you two be seemin' tight lately. I figure he would back you up. In a fightin' way, not a sex way."

"What you tryin' to say, nigga?"

Meanwhile, Halleigh had gotten up and turned her ass toward Scar. She was bending over in front of Scar, grinding her ass into his dick.

The energy in the room was frenetic. Scar was mad horny and about to fuck this chick, and Sticks and Day suddenly started beefing with each other. The music seemed to get louder and the beat seemed to quicken. Everyone was running at max energy.

Halleigh bent all the way over with her head between her knees. Scar had both his palms firmly planted on each of her ass cheeks, spreading them wide. Halleigh reached into the side of her mouth, between her gums and cheek, and pulled out a razor blade.

Sticks turned to Day to tell him to shut the fuck up. He cocked his fist to punch Day in the mouth at the same time that Halleigh spun around and swiped the razor blade at Scar's face.

Scar reacted quickly enough to avoid the razor blade. The razor's edge went sweeping an inch in front of his face.

Sticks held back his punch when he saw the commotion between Halleigh and Scar. Scar, on the other hand, didn't hold back his punch. As soon as he avoided the blade, he punched Halleigh in her jaw as hard as he could. This sent her flying across the room, and her cheek and jaw immediately started swelling.

By sheer instinct, Day instantly jumped up to protect Halleigh. He leaped across the room and landed on top of her. His intent was to cover her and protect her from any more punches.

Scar came over and tried to get at Halleigh. He was wildly throwing punches at her and threatening to kill her. Day was trying to get in the way of Scar's punches, but a few were landing. Day realized he couldn't protect her without Scar becoming suspicious. He had to make it look like he was trying to restrain her. He had to get her out of there quickly.

He picked her up off the floor and slammed her up against the wall. He held her by her throat, looked her in the eyes, and mouthed the word "Sorry" before he punched her in the stomach. She doubled over in agony.

"I'll take this bitch out of here," Day said to Scar.

"Fuck that. I want this bitch dead." Scar pulled out his gun and aimed it at Halleigh.

"Hold up, hold up." Day stepped in front of the gun. "You don't need blood on yo' hands right now. Let me take this bitch. I'll kill her and dump the body."

Scar kept his gun pointed as he thought about it. "Yeah, a'ight. Kill this bitch." He lowered his gun and gave Halleigh one last punch to the face. "Fuckin' bitch." Then he spat on her.

Sticks was just standing there doing nothing. He was sort of enjoying watching Scar beat this chick. He liked that this prostitute had enough heart to go after Scar. That was his kind of girl. Too bad she was about to die.

"Sticks, you stay here, mu'fucka. How the fuck you bring some grimy bitch up in here? You gots some explaining to do. You done fucked up twice now. If I don't like what I hear, you gon' die too." He pointed his gun at Sticks.

Day wished he could stay around and watch Sticks try to squirm his way out of this one, but he needed to get Halleigh far away from there. Scar was focused on Sticks, so now was the perfect time to get ghost. He put

Halleigh in a choke hold and pushed her out the door without saying a word.

Halleigh struggled to release herself from Day's hold as he shuffled her to his SUV. Not wanting to have to run around the streets of Baltimore naked, she got in the front seat of the Escalade. As soon as Day got in the driver's side, she started hitting him.

"You fucking asshole!" She was swinging wildly without any aim, mainly connecting with his arm.

"Relax." He attempted to stop her punches as he sped away.

"Why did you hit me?"

"I was protecting you. Now, stop before we crash." He was doing his best to block the uneven punches.

Halleigh realized her punches were ineffective, and she really didn't want to crash, so she stopped her attack on Dayvid.

"Thank you," he said.

Halleigh watched the world whiz by the passenger's side window. She was mad at Dayvid. She could have taken care of Scar if he hadn't gotten in the way. She'd taken a beating before at the hands of her old pimp, Manolo. It was nothing she couldn't have handled.

They rode in silence down I-95 for about twenty minutes, until Day pulled over at a rest stop. After he parked the car he turned to her.

"I'm sorry I hit you."

"I don't give a fuck. It didn't hurt anyway. You a pussy." She wouldn't face him.

Day saw that she obviously wasn't going to accept an apology, so he would try to talk some sense into her.

"What the fuck were you thinking? You could have gotten yourself killed!" He raised his voice.

"Don't act like my father. I know what I'm doing." She turned to him and matched his volume.

"You think a little bitty razor blade is going to kill him? You are fucking crazy. Let me handle it."

"I did let you handle it, and you ain't done shit. At least I'm doing something about it."

"I told you I'm working on it. Just stay out of it." They were fully screaming at each other at this point.

"Fuck you! You need my help, and now all of a sudden you want me to stay out of it? This nigga needs to die."

"I'll handle it!"

"I bet you will. What, you wanna fuck Scar? Is that it? You wanna become Scar's bitch?" she taunted.

"The fuck you talking about?"

"You know what I'm talkin' about. You coming over to my house all the time, I just danced for y'all, and now I'm sitting here butt-ass naked, and you haven't so much as looked at me or tried to push up on me. Seems to me you want to fuck Scar instead."

Day had been checking Halleigh out when she was dancing, but he was more consumed with his rage and jealousy than thinking about fucking Halleigh. He looked now at Halleigh sitting there in her thong and it got him aroused. Her body was better than he had ever envisioned it. Her breasts were still firm even without a bra, and her skin was perfectly smooth.

"You want to get fucked. Is that what this is about?" He looked directly in her eyes.

"I'm sitting here naked and you ain't doing nothing."

There was a slight pause for the tension to build, and then they couldn't hold back anymore. The tension broke; they leaned toward each other and began feverishly kissing. Dayvid's hands greedily roamed over every inch of Halleigh's body. They had both been waiting for this moment for a long time. She hungrily unbuckled his belt, unzipped his pants, and reached in for his manhood. His dick was rock hard, and Halleigh couldn't wait to see it unleashed.

They slid into the back seat, and Dayvid got on top of Halleigh. She pulled his pants down and started stroking his cock. Dayvid ripped off her panties and plunged two fingers into her hole. She moaned with delight the second his fingers hit her wet pussy. Dayvid was sucking her breasts and fingering her flower while she was stroking his hard, hot dick. She couldn't wait any longer.

"I need you inside me." She spread her legs wider as she guided his manhood to her pussy.

Dayvid slid his cock deep inside her. It felt so good to both of them. Her pussy lips wrapped tight around his dick as he rapidly stroked in and out of her.

Halleigh had not felt pleasure like this in a long time. It kind of hurt when he was all the way in, but Halleigh loved it. The more he stroked, the wetter she got. Dayvid loved how wet and tight Halleigh was. Both of them had wanted this for so long. So much sexual tension had been building toward this that they couldn't hold it any longer.

"I'm going to cum!" she screamed.

"Me too!"

Together they exploded in orgasm. Afterward, they both lay there for a while, panting, trying to catch their breath. It may not have been the longest fuck session, but it was the most intense. It was animalistic. It was complete passion that was long overdue.

They lay there looking at each other, consumed with post-sex glow. Both were in ecstasy but also shocked by what had just happened.

"Wow," Dayvid said.

"Yeah." She smiled.

"You're going to have to disappear for a while. You can't be seen anywhere."

"I know."

They kissed each other passionately.

"I'll tell Scar that I shot you and dumped your body in the bay." He softly rubbed her cheek where she had been hit by the back of his hand.

They kissed again.

"Now will you finally kill Scar?" she asked.

"Is that what this was about? You fucked me to get me to kill Scar?" Dayvid was offended.

"You're still not going to do it?"

Their bliss from a few seconds ago was now turning into another argument.

"You think just 'cause you fucked me, I'll suddenly kill Scar now? How fucking dumb you think I am?"

"What the fuck are you so scared of? I just put my ass on the line, and you too bitch-ass to do anything." She started to wriggle out from underneath him.

"You too stupid to realize what I'm trying to do."

"Fuck you. Take my ass home. I can't believe I just fucked a bitch like you." She climbed into the front seat.

"Fuck you too. You got no sense, bitch." He pulled up his pants and slid into the driver's seat. He wished he could make her walk home, but he would never do that to her. When it came to Halleigh, Dayvid had a hard time being an asshole.

Dayvid drove back to Halleigh's house without looking at her or saying a word to her. She did the same thing to him. They weren't going to see eye to eye on the situation with Scar. Dayvid wanted to tell her not to go after Scar again, but he figured there was no point in even trying, because she wouldn't listen.

He had barely stopped in Halleigh's driveway before she jumped out and ran to her front door. He rolled the window down and yelled to her as she ran, "Stay out of sight."

"Fuck you." She ran inside her house and slammed the door.

Chapter 11

Time Limit

Scar stood with his feet wide, arm extended straight out in front of him, holding his gun. Sticks was sitting on the couch, staring down the barrel of the gun. He had been telling Scar the story of how he met Halleigh, or Sincere, as she told him her name was. He recounted how he had run into her at the diner and then again at the bodega a few days later. The mention of the meeting with Chief Hill didn't help the situation. Scar was still so enraged by the thought of losing that money that he was on the verge of shooting Sticks for bringing it up again. Sticks was on thin ice, and if he didn't satisfy Scar with his story and convince him of his innocence, he was about to take his last breath.

Sticks rambled on and on. "I'm telling you. I had no idea. This bitch seemed like she was itching to get fucked. I know you been feelin' bad, so I brought her for you to cheer you up. I mean, I wanted to fuck her, but not until you had her. I mean, if she was down for a train, I was cool with that too. I'll do whatever you want. You gotta believe me. I had no idea this ho be trippin' like that." He was afraid that if and when he stopped talking, he would be shot.

When he finished with his explanation, he looked at Scar, who had been standing quietly listening to him babble. Scar said nothing. Sticks didn't know if this was a good thing or a bad thing. Was he not asking questions because he was satisfied with the story? Was he not asking questions because he was fed up and didn't believe a word? The not knowing was stressing Sticks out to the point that his eyes started to water. His heart was beating a mile a minute, and he actually started praying silently to God, something he hadn't done since he was a little boy. If ever there was a time that Sticks needed the Lord to hear him, now was the time.

Sitting there waiting for Scar to make some sort of decision and do something felt like an eternity. In actuality, it had only been about two minutes. Finally, Scar had made his decision.

"Get ready to meet your maker, mu'fucka," he snarled.

Bang! Scar pulled the trigger and fired the gun. Sticks let out a scream. The bullet sped toward Sticks and landed in the wall above his head.

Sticks paused to take inventory of his body. Scar had missed; he was still alive. He looked to Scar with his eyes open wide. He was at a loss for words. He didn't know if he should thank Scar or curse him.

"Next time you fuck up, I won't miss." Scar put away his gun and left the room.

Sticks just sat there panting like he had just run a marathon. His adrenaline was so high he felt as if he might have a heart attack. His nerves were shot. He started to cry a little bit after Scar left. That was it for Sticks; he now knew he had to go out on his own. He needed to be his own boss.

Fuck Scar, he thought as he wiped the tears from his eyes. Scar and Sticks were now enemies. The next time Sticks and Scar saw each other would be when Sticks was putting a gun to Scar's head.

***

Dayvid Sped away from Halleigh's house headed toward Baltimore. He was confused about what had just happened between them. He thought the sex had happened because there was a mutual attraction and their passion had built up so much that it had to be unleashed. The way she reacted afterward and the things she said to him, though, made him think she had other motives. She was using sex to manipulate him. This pissed him off. He had started to have feelings for Halleigh that went beyond sex, but it seemed she wasn't feeling the same way.

Day drove through the empty streets of Baltimore. It was the middle of the night, all the stores were closed, and no one was on the streets except an occasional corner boy hoping to make his last few dollars before he called it a night. Every time one of them saw Day driving up the block, they would perk up, thinking it could be the sale they were waiting for.

Day was driving around trying to clear his head. It had been an emotional few days, and he needed to put it all in perspective so he didn't do something stupid and get himself killed. Acting on his emotions right now would be a bad mistake. He needed to think rationally and stick to his plan. No matter how much pressure he was feeling, he needed to stay calm and focused.

He felt like he was close to his goal. If he could just get his contacts and connections all in place, he would have enough money to fund his own operation, and then he could take Scar out. It all seemed so fragile to him. One wrong move and it could all fall to pieces.

Halleigh was scaring him a bit. He couldn't understand why she wouldn't trust him. He had a plan that he thought was tight. She just needed to trust him and let him execute it, and then they would be taken care of. Instead, she was becoming impatient and reckless. She didn't seem to understand that she was tempting fate and knocking on death's door, putting them both in danger when she pulled stunts like the one she pulled earlier.

Day was tired. After driving around and calming himself down, he was ready to go home and sleep for the next week. He was driving down his street, thinking about his comfortable bed and about to pull up in front of his crib when his phone rang. He didn't recognize the number, so he ignored the call. The caller immediately called back. Again he ignored the call. Whoever was on the other line was persistent, because they called back instantly. Day angrily answered the phone.

"What?"

"Why you ain't answer?" It was Scar calling.

Day didn't recognize the number because Scar changed his phones like he changed his underwear. He was always trying to stay one step ahead of the law.

Quickly changing his tone, he said, "Oh yo, I didn't know it was you. What up?"

"You do that thing?"

"Yeah, it's done. Fishes probably be eatin' well in the harbor tonight," Day said.

"Good. Fuck that bitch. Now go talk to Derek."

"Now?"

"When the fuck you think I'm talking about? Yeah, now."

"I'm mad tired, boss," Day replied.

"I don't give a fuck. I'm awake, you're awake. Go do it. If you don't, don't bother coming back here," Scar warned.

Scar was being unrealistic and demanding, but Day had no choice. He had to go. He couldn't take the chance of not being allowed back to the Dirty Money

Crew. He had worked hard to establish himself solidly within the crew, and he didn't want to ruin it all because of this one little thing.

"Okay, boss. I'm on my way."

"Right choice. I'm sick of y'all fuckin' up lately. Niggas are gonna start payin' around here." Scar didn't wait for an answer. He hung up.

Day was tired, angry, and getting sick of Scar's bullshit. He wanted to get this over and done with so he could get some much needed sleep. Derek better not start playing games, because Day was not going to be in the mood.

He called Derek on his cell. Derek was not happy to be woken up.

"Fuller," Derek answered groggily.

"Time to meet."

"Who is this?"

"It's Day, mu'fucka. Time to pay the piper."

"The fuck you want?" Derek was more alert now.

"An update. You and me be meetin' now."

"Ah, shit. I was sleeping." Derek was stalling. He had nothing to tell them.

"I don't care."

"Now? Where?" Derek instantly started making mental notes of what he had to do before this meeting.

"The Pagoda, Patterson Park. Come alone or your kids won't see tomorrow." Day disconnected the call. Each man was coming to this meeting tired and angry.

Derek became furious and frantic. He rushed to put on clothes and make the necessary call to the officer who was assisting him.

Day entered the park from East Baltimore Avenue and made his way toward the pagoda. There was a stand of trees near the pagoda that provided cover for him as he waited. He scanned the area and saw no sign of Derek. He didn't have the patience for this bullshit right now. He was going to sit down against a tree and close his eyes for fifteen minutes. If Derek wasn't there when he opened them, he was leaving.

Day was in a deep sleep when he was startled awake by a sound. He jumped to his feet and pulled out his gun. Careful to stay close to the tree, he crouched and searched the area for the source of the sound. He had no idea how long he had been asleep.

The sun had just started to rise, and his eyes were having trouble adjusting to the light. Finally, Day saw Derek coming from the opposite side of the pagoda. He waited and watched to make sure that no one else had come and he was not being set up.

Satisfied that Derek was alone, Day came out from behind the tree, pointing his gun at Derek. "Put your hands away from your body."

Derek saw the gun and obeyed the command as Day approached him. He stretched his hands away from his body like he was on the cross. Day made him turn away and then patted him down. Finding no weapon, Day told him to lower his arms and put away his own gun.

"What took you so long?" Day asked.

"You woke my ass up," Derek replied.

"You do what Scar wanted you to do?"

"I talked to the mayor. He's willing to help, but it's gonna cost you," Derek lied.

"Fuck that. If you don't hurry up, it's gonna cost you."

"What's that supposed to mean?" Derek narrowed his eyes in rage.

"It means the clock be ticking on yo kids," Day said smugly.

In a rage, Derek lunged at Day and tackled him. The two men started wrestling and punching each other. Day managed to throw Derek off of him, get to his feet, and draw his gun. Derek flipped over. Seeing the gun pointed directly at him, he remained frozen, hoping that Day wouldn't shoot.

"Back the fuck up!" Day commanded and Derek obliged. "You got one week, mu'fucka. If you don't deliver, then you gon' start seeing your kids' body parts one by one."

Day didn't dare turn his back on Derek. Keeping his gun drawn, he walked backward away from Derek, who stayed motionless on the ground, burning with anger. When he was far enough away, Day turned and quickly left the park. Derek sat there watching him and vowing that he would get revenge on Day, Scar, and anyone else who was involved in the kidnapping of his children.

Derek had enlisted the help of one of Chief Hill's officers, who had been waiting in an unmarked car outside the park. He pulled out his phone and called the officer.

"The suspect is headed out the north side of the park toward East Baltimore Ave."

"Copy," the officer responded.

"Follow him, but do not engage. I will meet up with you ASAP." He hung up the phone.

Derek was going to get to Scar and save his children through Day. He didn't know how yet, but he was sure that he would figure it out. He had to; he only had a week.

Chapter 12

Confess

Day was amped after his showdown with Derek. Unaware that he was now being followed, he sped off from the park. The sun had risen and the city was waking up. People were coming out of their homes and heading off to work. All the hustlers were getting back to their corners for another day of slinging rock.

He drove through the city planning his next move. Reporting this meeting to Scar could wait. First he needed to find Flex and hear his version of the events at the diner. Day knew what he'd seen, and he didn't believe Chief Hill really stole Scar's money, but he wanted to see what Flex had to say about it.

Day stopped at home to change his clothes before finding Flex. He rushed through the front door and stripped off his clothes, heading straight to the shower. The hot water felt good streaming down his muscular back. He stood in his shower letting the water beat down on him and wash away the stress that had been piling up on his shoulders. He had been feeling pressure from everyone in his life lately. Standing there in the heat and steam, he started to let go of that pressure.

He thought back to his teenage years, his friend Malek, and the lessons Malek had taught him: how to be a man, how to take care of yourself and your business, and the most important one, how to take care of the one you love. Halleigh and Malek Jr. had been the ones that Malek loved, and Dayvid had vowed to look out for them.

Dayvid was feeling guilty about having sex with his dead friend's girl, but it just happened, and now it was done. He looked up to the heavens as the water poured down, and said a prayer to his fallen friend, asking for his forgiveness.

Day watched himself in the mirror as he dried off after his long, hot shower. He admired his cut physique and promised himself to get back to the gym and lift some weights. With everything happening in his life, he had been neglecting his normal workout routine. He needed to be in top form with everything that was about to go down. He figured there would be some hand to hand combat happening, and he couldn't afford to come out on the losing end of those battles.

Day wrapped the towel around his waist, went into his bedroom, and sat down on the edge of the bed for a second. The next thing he knew, he was lying back on the bed, closing his eyes. In an instant, he was sound asleep.

Meanwhile, the police officer who had followed him was sitting in his car out front. As he waited for Day to come out, Derek called him.

"What's the word?" Derek asked.

"Followed the suspect to a house. Suspect entered. Now I'm waiting for him to emerge," the officer replied.

"Good. Keep a close eye on him. Let me know when he's on the move."

"Copy."

Seven hours later, Day shot straight up into a sitting position. He was startled awake by a nightmare he was having in which Halleigh was being tortured. This made Day very uncomfortable. Maybe it was a sign and she was really in trouble.

He rushed to his phone and started to call her, but then hung up. Halleigh had made it perfectly clear the last time she saw him that she didn't want his help.

If that's the way she wants it, then so be it, he thought. *She doesn't think she needs my help, so she ain't getting it. Besides, it's just a dream. I'm sure it's nothing.*

Refreshed and refocused, Day got dressed quickly. He was feeling a sense of urgency, like something wasn't right, like time was running out. But running out on what? He had felt in control before, but with recent circumstances, he felt that control slipping a bit. He had to act fast. His life depended on it.

He left the house in search of Flex. There were a few places that Flex might be at this hour. The one place he didn't want him to be was at Scar's hideout. He needed Flex to himself. Day might have to let Flex know that he saw what went down, and he didn't want to take the chance of Scar hearing.

As Day drove around the hood searching for Flex, he noticed that the energy on the streets was completely different. Earlier that morning, there were only a few people on their way to work and the stores were all just opening their doors. Now every corner had a fiend copping from a corner boy, the stores were all open and lit up, and most of the windows on the apartment buildings were bright with light. Inside the apartments, the working people were settling in to watch their favorite television shows before going to sleep and then doing it all again the next day.

Day drove to the first of Flex's corners and was told by one of his crew that Flex had just been there. Unaware that he was being followed, Day drove to the corner where Flex was supposed to be.

As he pulled up, Day's SUV attracted attention. Whenever a car crept up to a corner, everyone got on alert, especially when it was a shiny black Escalade with tints. It could be a potential customer or a rival. Either you would be making money, or you would be shooting and running for your life.

Flex was talking to one of the corner boys as he eyeballed the SUV. Day rolled down his passenger's side window as he pulled up to the corner.

"Ay yo, Flex," he called out.

Not knowing who was calling him, Flex stayed where he was and cautiously looked into the SUV. His demeanor changed when he saw that it was Day. His tension lifted and he smiled.

"What up, fam?" Flex approached the SUV, reached inside, and greeted Day by slapping palms with him.

"You got time? I need to talk some business." Day didn't want to spook Flex, so he was trying to act nonchalant.

"Yeah, you know, just keeping my blocks running smooth. I always got time for business. What's up?" Flex was leaning his elbows against the car door as he spoke.

"Get in. Let's take a ride."

Flex opened the door and got inside the luxury vehicle. Noticing the leather seats and custom stereo system he said, "This is nice. I'ma buy one of these someday."

"Word? How you gonna do that?" Day tried to lead him as he pulled away from the curb.

"I got some paper saved. Just waiting for my wallet to get a little thicker."

"I hear you. That's kind of what I wanted to talk to you about." Day kept his eyes on the road as he drove.

"I'm always down to make my wallet thicker. What is it?" Flex started fiddling with the stereo.

"Nah, it ain't about making your wallet thicker. It's about the thickness of it right now."

"What you mean?" Flex looked at Day out of the corner of his eye.

"Business been dropping off as of late, but somehow you got money stashed."

Flex defended himself. "What you implying? I'm frugal, dude. Don't be spending on stupid shit."

"Okay." Day kept his eyes on the road. He purposely kept his answer short and noncommittal in order to make Flex confused and nervous.

They continued driving as the energy inside the car completely changed. Flex just stared out the passenger's window, and Day could feel the nervous energy coming off of him. It was exactly what Day had hoped for: make Flex uncomfortable and get him to confess for fear he would be killed. Now he could really start to put on the pressure.

"How long it take you to save all that?"

"I don't know." Flex kept his face turned away from Day.

"How much you got?"

"I don't know."

"I know that's a lie, but that's your business. I feel you."

"Why you so interested? I keep that shit to myself because I don't want niggas tryin' to jack me for it." Flex finally turned toward Day.

"It's not really me who's interested."

"Then who is?"

"Scar."

That caught Flex off guard. He was hoping to be on Scar's radar, but he was getting the feeling that this wasn't a good thing.

Flex argued his case. "Yo, I give Scar his cut. I ain't never skimmed off the top."

"Well, see, that's where I think you two might differ on opinion."

"Fuck that! I'd never do some grimy shit like that!" Flex was adamant.

Day had Flex right where he wanted him. For effect, he pulled the SUV over so he could turn and give Flex his full attention. They were on a deserted pier in front of a warehouse overlooking the harbor. Day had chosen such a desolate spot to scare Flex into thinking he might be killed.

Day began, "Okay, listen. Sticks been tellin' Scar that Chief Hill stuck him up and stole money from him."

"That's fucked up. So what, we gonna kill Chief Hill?"

"Sticks said it happened the night he went to talk to the chief at the diner." Day waited to see what Flex would say to this. Flex said nothing.

Day continued, "See, I think shit didn't happen that way. But here's the thing, when I asked that nigga about it, he said he gave you the money. That you was gonna hold it and he didn't know what you did with it. He said he told Scar that story about the chief to protect you."

He looked Flex dead in the eyes and asked, "So, where's the fuckin' money? If Scar find out you stole from him . . ."

Knowing the answer, Flex cut him short. "Yo, that ain't what happened. Sticks was supposed to meet with the chief and he wanted me to be lookout. . . ." Flex proceeded to tell Day what happened that night, not leaving out one detail. He was going to make sure that

Day believed him, because he knew his life depended on it, and because he damn sure wasn't going to take the fall for Sticks. He was furious.

Getting Flex to confess was easier than Day had thought it would be. Day was prepared to tell Flex he had followed him and saw everything, but Flex was so shook that he gave it up without much coaxing. Now all Day had to do was to get him to tell Scar the story the way he wanted him to. He said, "If this is true, you need to let Scar know. He's already suspicious of that Chief Hill bullshit story, so you know Sticks gonna be runnin' like a bitch to Scar and change his story."

"I swear that is exactly how it went down. Sticks is a lying mu'fucka." Flex felt like he was pleading for his life.

"Then we go tell Scar before Sticks gets to him."

Still oblivious to the officer who had been following him since leaving his house earlier, Day started his SUV and pulled away, headed for Scar's hideout.

Chapter 13

The Truth Will Set You Free

The officer who was following Day was making sure to stay far enough away to remain undetected. After leaving the pier and heading up Broening Highway, the officer pulled out his cell phone and called Detective Fuller.

"Fuller." Derek answered.

"Sir, subject just left Holabird Industrial, now heading north. He has picked up another African American male. Should I keep on them?"

"Stay with them. I'll come relieve you soon."

Derek had been looking for his kids all day. Every lead he followed was a dead end, and his frustration was at its peak. He was tracking down this one last lead, and then he would give the officer a break. He had earned it, and Derek could hear in his voice that he was getting bored with his assignment. Derek knew that could only lead to one thing—the officer getting careless and losing sight of the subject.

On the ride over to see Scar, Flex started getting nervous. He was afraid that the truth wouldn't work.

"Yo, I don't know if Scar gonna like my story. Maybe we need to tell him something else."

"What?"

"I just don't think he'll believe me. Let's tell him some-thin' else." Flex's nerves were making him talk fast.

"Just tell him your story."

"I'll tell him my story, but how 'bout I add some-thin'? You know, make me look better."

"Nigga, you look fine from your story. Sticks the one who look like shit." Day didn't need Flex going off script now.

"Nah, I know, but how 'bout I tell him, like, I chased the chief and caught him and got some of the money back? Then I can give him what Sticks gave me. Both me and Sticks won't look so bad."

"That is some dumb-ass shit. Sticks tryin'a play you, fool. That nigga don't care 'bout you. What if Scar find out you lyin'?"

"I'm just sayin'. That way it won't look like I was tryin'a steal from him."

"Nigga, just tell him the truth and say you ain't had no idea what was goin' on. You start makin' shit up, you won't be able to keep yo' lies straight. Scar catch you slippin' with yo' lies and both of us get dead."

Flex remained quiet. He thought over the lecture Day had just given him. He was confused. He thought Sticks was cool and was having trouble believing that he would play him like that. There were still a lot of lessons that Flex needed to learn. It seemed like Day might be the one to teach him.

"You right. I'll just tell him how it really went down."

They drove the rest of the way in silence.

Flex started trembling as they pulled up to Scar's hideout. Day noticed this and knew he needed to get this kid in the right frame of mind. If Flex walked in there and started fucking up his story, it would be lights out for both of them. Day was bringing Flex in front of Scar and taking responsibility for him. He was vouching for this young buck, and if Scar didn't believe him or didn't like what he was hearing, they were done.

"Get yo head on, nigga! You go in there shaking like a bitch and Scar gonna murk us both."

"I'm good. I'm good." Flex was still trembling.

"Nigga, I mean it. Stop yo quakin'." Day punched Flex in his face, connecting with his jaw. This seemed to wake Flex up and stopped him from shaking.

"You right. The truth shall set you free. Right, nigga?" Flex smiled and stepped out of the car, ready to tell his story and deal with the consequences like a man.

Day watched him walk to the entrance and said to himself, "Young buck about to become a grown-ass man."

A haze of weed smoke and a pounding bass beat from the stereo greeted them as they walked into the front room. There were women in various states of undress all over, and each girl was entertaining one of Scar's henchmen. Some were just dancing for their man; others were fully fucking them. It seemed Scar had put together a little party—or an orgy, depending on how you looked at it.

Even with all of the partying going on, Flex still couldn't really let loose. He was focused on telling Scar his story and saving his ass. Doubt crept into his mind, though, when he saw the party. Maybe this wasn't the best time to tell Scar the bad news. Maybe he should wait.

He looked at Day and gave him a look that asked, *What now?*

Day sensed Flex's apprehension. He didn't care about interrupting the party. He needed Scar to hear this information.

"No time like the present." Day put his hand on Flex's back and started guiding him toward Scar, who was sitting on the couch, fucking around with the finest girl in the room.

"Ay yo, Scar. Can I holla at you?" Flex said.

Scar ignored him and continued kissing the girl and caressing her smooth skin and plump, round ass. Flex just stood there watching, with Day right at his side. Day was not about to leave Flex alone now. He was so close to finally getting Scar to see Sticks for what he was; he wasn't about to let this opportunity slip by.

"Ay yo, Scar," Flex said a little louder.

Scar kissed the girl for a few more seconds then pulled away and addressed the two men. "Can't you see I'm busy? You two freaks get off watching? There's plenty of girls. Go get yourselves one and leave me the fuck alone." He started sucking the girl's bare breasts.

"I need to speak to you. It's important," Flex persisted.

"You gon' want to hear what he got to say," Day chimed in.

Realizing the two weren't going to leave him alone, Scar stopped his seduction. The girl remained sitting on his lap as Scar looked at the two men with an annoyed look on his face.

"Okay. What?"

"I think we should go somewhere a little more private and less loud," Day suggested.

"I'll make that decision. Now, what the fuck is this about?" Scar said.

"Chief Hill didn't steal your money," Flex stated plainly.

This caught Scar off guard and got his attention. He didn't want it to look like it affected him, but it did. He sat there with no expression on his face, trying to conceal his confusion. If the chief didn't steal the money, then where was it? Who had it? Scar needed answers.

"Get up," he said to the woman on his lap. As she stood, he smacked her ass and she strutted away like a model on the runway. Scar directed his attention back to the two soldiers.

"Let's go in the back room." He stood from the couch and made his way from the party, with Day and Flex following.

Scar sat at his desk as the faint sounds of the party in the next room came through the walls. Flex and Day were standing side by side in the middle of the room, facing Scar. They looked like two boys standing before the principal, about to tell on the school bully.

Scar studied their faces, looking for any sign that they were scheming. After sufficiently asserting his power and letting them know who was in control of this situation, Scar asked, "So, what is it you have to say?"

Flex began, "I've heard that Sticks is sayin' Chief Hill took money from him the night they met at the diner. That ain't the truth." He then retold his story from the beginning—everything from the start of the day, when they followed the chief in front of the courthouse, to the end of the night, when Sticks gave him the money and told him to keep it quiet. As he did with Day, he didn't leave out one detail.

Scar sat at his desk taking in every word. His facial expression remained completely neutral throughout the entire tale. "Why are you telling me this?" he asked when Flex finished his story.

Flex looked at Day with a puzzled expression. He didn't really know how to answer the question. He figured the answer was obvious—because he was trying to save his own ass and because Sticks was being a sneaky motherfucker who stole from Scar.

Scar continued, "I'm just sayin', if you hadn't told me, I woulda never known that Sticks lied to me. How you know Sticks was sayin' that story anyway—unless you were in on it?"

Scar pulled a gun from his desk and pointed it at Flex. He was heated that someone had lied and stolen from him, especially one of his own men. The story didn't add up to him, and he suspected that Flex was lying as well. Someone was going to pay for their disrespect and disloyalty.

"Whoa, hold on, boss. I told him what Sticks was sayin'." Thinking quick on his feet, Day started making up a story on the spot.

"I ran into Chief Hill and stuck my fuckin' gun in his ribs. I was gonna murk his ass for stealing from us. But when I asked him where the money was, that nigga kept sayin' he didn't steal it. The thing is, he looked so shook I thought he was 'bout to shit on his self, and I started to believe he really ain't know nothin' about that shit. I didn't wanna have a cop killing on my hands, so I let the bitch go. I figured I could always get to the chief again later if I needed to.

"So I go ask Sticks about it, and he says he really gave the money to Flex to hold on to, and he don't know what Flex did with it. He says he told you that shit about Chief Hill to protect Flex. But see, that don't really add up to me. Why would he give Flex the money instead of givin' it back to you?

"So I go ask Flex about it, and he tells me his story. I told him to come tell you." He paused for a minute. He was just making things up as he went along and talking so fast that he wasn't even really sure what he had just said. He couldn't tell from Scar's expression if he believed the story, but there was no turning back now.

"Boss, Sticks been playin' you."

"Yeah, I ain't lyin', Scar. I'm telling you the truth," Flex added.

Scar lowered his gun. "Where the fuck is my money?"

"I still got it," Flex said nervously. "I can give you what Sticks gave to me. He got the rest, like I said."

"Mu'fucka, you damn right you gon' gimme my money back." Scar stood and came out from behind his desk, still holding his gun.

"I can go get my share now, boss."

Scar approached Flex. He raised his gun and pressed it against Flex's temple. Flex stood frozen, waiting for his certain death. Day watched with wide eyes, afraid to make any move.

"Nah, nigga, you gon' bring all my money back. First you gon' get Sticks to give you his share, then you gon' murk that snake." Scar took the gun from Flex's temple and held it out to hand it to him.

Flex couldn't believe it. He felt like he was getting a second chance on his life, even though he technically didn't do anything wrong. Thankful to be alive and willing to do whatever it took to stay that way, Flex said, "Consider it already done." He took the gun from Scar and put it in his waistband.

"You gon' earn yo stripes, youngin'. If it ain't done in twenty-four hours, you best start making your funeral arrangements." Scar walked out of the room and back to the party, leaving the two standing there counting their blessings to still be alive.

Sticks was about to die at the hands of a young buck who was eager to prove himself. This couldn't have worked out any better for Day. He ratted Sticks out without having to do it himself or give away that he had seen the whole thing go down. Even though they had been fighting, his first thought was that he had to tell Halleigh his good fortune.

"You best get on that," Day said to Flex.

"Sticks about to breathe his last breath," Flex snarled.

"Let's go. Time's running out."

They walked out of the room, through the party, and out the front door.

Chapter 14

A Taste for Blood

Flex was pacing back and forth in his apartment. He was sorting out how he was going to lure Sticks into a trap. He knew the location where he wanted to meet him, an abandoned barn up in horse country, but he didn't want to tip Sticks off that something was up.

This was an important step for him and he knew it. Flex was relatively new to the game, and he had never actually killed anyone. Killing Sticks would instantly enhance his reputation on the street and solidify his position in the Dirty Money Crew. It had to be done right, and it had to be done soon.

On the ride over to his crib, Day had given Flex some suggestions on what to say to Sticks. Flex liked what Day had suggested, and he was now trying to make sure he had it all straight. Day offered to help Flex with the kill, but Flex declined, feeling that he needed to do it himself. So here he was, psyching himself up to literally and figuratively end his first life. He would be ending Sticks' life for real, and ending the life he knew before becoming a murderer. After it was done, he could never look back.

Flex snorted several bumps of coke to make sure he was in the right frame of mind for the job. Sufficiently coked up, he called Sticks.

***

After getting Sticks to agree to meet him, Flex jumped in his car and immediately drove north. His plan depended on the element of surprise, so he wanted to make sure he was there before Sticks.

Sitting amongst the horse stables and hay bales, Flex continued psyching himself up by doing more and more coke. He started shadow boxing and swinging a two-by-four like a bat to release some of the energy the coke had created in his body. He kept looking out the broken window for Sticks and checking the gun to make sure it was loaded. Anything to keep himself occupied. His adrenaline was maxed out. He was high as shit, and paranoia started to overtake him.

As Flex was throwing stones in the air and hitting them with the two-by-four like baseballs, the lights of a car came through the window. Flex stopped his game and peeked out the window. He recognized the car coming up to the barn as Sticks'. He pulled out the baggie of coke, did one last bump, and watched to make sure that Sticks was alone.

The car stopped, and Sticks got out of the driver's side. Flex didn't see anyone else with him, so he placed the two-by-four by the entrance and walked out front to meet Sticks.

"Ay yo, fam," he called out to Sticks as they walked toward one another to clasp hands and bump shoulders in a greeting.

"What's good?" Sticks replied. "You must be shook, nigga, havin' me come all the way out here."

"You know, I wanted to talk to you away from prying eyes. Not really trustin' Scar right now. Also wanted to show you where I'ma do Chief Hill. Make sure it's the right kind of place. You know I ain't never killed no one before."

"Word? You 'bout to lose yo murdering virginity? Damn, that's crazy. Can I watch you do it?" Sticks was amused by the information.

"I might need your help."

"Hell yeah. I'll gladly drop that mu'fuckin' chief."

"Well, yeah, I might need your help with that, but I was talking about help with Scar. This nigga be buggin'. I think he be thinkin' I stole money from him," Flex said.

"Oh shit. Why you think that?"

"Just some shit he said when he told me to murk Chief Hill." Flex was trying to be as vague as possible.

"I feel you. He definitely buggin' lately."

"I ain't sure I want to be with that nigga no more." Flex was reeling Sticks in.

This was exactly the type of shit Sticks wanted to hear. He was hoping to recruit Flex, and now it seemed as though Flex was asking to be recruited. Sticks was going to take this opportunity and start to build his army.

"For real, I been havin' problems with Scar's disrespecting ass for a while. I'm ready to step out on my own. I set some shit in motion, so Scar won't be around to disrespect us too much longer. I'm lookin' for good soldiers to come with."

"Yo, I'm down. I seen how you roll when you hit me off with that nice chunk of change at the diner." Flex put up his hand to slap Sticks' hand in a sign of solidarity.

"That's what I'm talkin' 'bout. Let's make our own money." Sticks slapped hands with Flex.

"Let's celebrate. I got some clean yayo in the barn."

"Let's do this." Sticks started walking toward the entrance to the barn, excited to have a partner in crime.

When they got to the entrance, Flex grabbed the two-by-four. Sticks saw some odd movement by Flex out of the corner of his eye, but before he could turn around, it was too late. Flex cocked the board back like he had been doing while he was waiting and swung the two-by-four as hard as he could. The impact opened a huge gash in the back of Sticks' head and sent him crumbling to the ground, unconscious.

Flex checked Sticks' pulse. He was alive, which was a good thing because Flex still needed to find out where the rest of Scar's money was. While Sticks was unconscious, Flex tied his wrists together and hung him by the rafters, his feet just barely off the ground. His arms were extended over his head, and he was hanging in the middle of the barn like a heavy bag at a boxing gym.

When Sticks finally started to regain consciousness, the first thing Flex did was punch him as hard as he could in the stomach. It knocked the wind out of Sticks, causing him to spit up blood.

"Untie me, muthafucka." Sticks spat blood at Flex.

"You tryin' to set me up, huh, nigga?" Flex balled his fist and cracked Sticks in his mouth, loosening a few of his teeth and causing more blood to flow from his mouth and down his chin.

"The fuck you talkin' about?" Sticks was trying to clear his mouth of blood, spitting it to the floor.

"You stealin' money from Scar and tellin' Day I had it." Flex picked up the two-by-four and smacked Sticks across the kneecaps. If the sound was any indication, his kneecaps had been shattered. Sticks let out an agonizing scream.

Barely able to speak because of the pain, Sticks replied, "I don't know what you talkin' about."

Flex swung the board and connected with Sticks' ribs. Another scream came roaring from Sticks. He had broken ribs now and was having trouble breathing.

Laboring to breathe, he forced words from his mouth. "Okay, stop. . . . I took money . . . from Scar . . . but I never said . . . nothin' . . . 'bout you."

"Don't lie to me, mu'fucka." Flex began laying into Sticks' body with his fists, giving him repeated body blows like a boxer hitting a heavy bag. Sticks screamed in agony with every blow.

When he was finished and tired from his workout, Flex took a step back and examined the damage he had done. Sticks hung there with his head drooped down, covered in blood, exhausted from the beating he was taking.

"Now, I know you were tryin'a set me up. Day told me. So tell me where the rest of the money at," Flex said.

Unable to lift his head, Sticks began, "Day lyin'. . . . I ain't . . . set you up. Money . . . gone."

Flex couldn't afford to beat him anymore without risking killing him, so he resisted punching Sticks. "Come on. Just tell me where the money at."

"It's . . . gone." Sticks tried lifting his head and spitting at Flex again, but he didn't have the strength and ended up spitting on himself.

"I like your heart, bro. I seriously don't want to kill you, and I won't—if you just tell me where the money is."

Sticks didn't have energy to say anything this time. He just slowly shook his head.

Flex pulled out his gun and shot Sticks in the foot. Another blood-curdling scream filled the air. Flex couldn't believe the beating this guy was enduring.

"Come on, man. Scar told me to spare your life if you just return the money. He don't want no other problems right now. He got enough on his plate with the police on his ass. Don't make me shoot your other foot."

Barely audible now, Sticks started to speak. All he said was, "My . . . basement," as blood leaked from his mouth, head, and foot.

"That wasn't so hard, was it? Now, let me untie you," Flex replied.

"Thank you," Sticks whispered.

"You dumb mu'fucka. You really think I'm gonna let you go?" Flex mocked Sticks before he pointed the gun at his temple and pulled the trigger. The shot echoed through the barn. It blew a hole right through Sticks head and sent brain matter and blood flying through the air.

Flex stared in disbelief. He had just shot and killed his first human. It was easier than he expected, and it actually gave him a rush. He pulled out his baggie of coke, took a bump, and prepared to bury Sticks.

Chapter 15

Bliss Interrupted

Dayvid drove straight to Halleigh's house. He couldn't wait to tell her the good news—Scar had ordered Flex to kill Sticks. This would open up a straight path to Scar. He would be even closer to Scar now that Sticks was gone. There was less work for them to do, and the end of their revenge plot was in sight.

As soon as he pulled in the driveway, his excitement faded. The argument they had the last time they saw each other came slamming back to his memory. Although he was excited about the news and wanted to get past their argument, he wasn't sure how she would react. He tried to tell himself that he didn't care about her and that she could go out on her own, but now, the butterflies in his stomach told him he felt more for her than he admitted.

Dayvid rang the doorbell to the house and waited anxiously. The longer he stood there, the more he had to talk himself out of turning around and leaving. He rang the doorbell a few more times and was about to walk away when he finally saw Halleigh peeking out the side window. He couldn't punk out now.

Halleigh flung the door open. "Are you crazy ringing my bell like that? You're going to wake M.J.," she scolded.

"Sorry."

Halleigh just shook her head, left the door open, and walked away. Dayvid followed her into the house and into the kitchen. Halleigh was sitting at the table when he entered.

"What do you want?" She scowled at him.

Dayvid pulled up a chair.

"I didn't tell you you could sit," Halleigh snapped.

Dayvid calmly stood up and pushed the chair back in. He didn't want to start out fighting, so he obeyed her command without any backtalk.

"I just came by to tell you that Sticks is about to die," he said.

"Good. He deserves it." Halleigh stayed calm. Inside she was ecstatic, but she was still mad at Dayvid, so she didn't show any outward emotion. She hated the way Sticks acted toward her when she was pretending to be Sincere, like she was just some piece of meat that he owned.

"This is great news, Halleigh, and that's all you have to say? You don't want to know how or why?"

"Okay, how? Why?" she asked sarcastically.

Dayvid proceeded to tell her how it all came about. As he was telling the story, he sat down without thinking. Halleigh was so caught up that she didn't really notice. She couldn't believe how everything worked out.

"Damn, you played all them fools," she said with a smile. "So, what do we do now?"

"We go after Scar immediately. Once Sticks is dead, we make our play for Scar and blame it on Sticks. We can say that Sticks heard Scar was after him, so he acted first and ordered one of his corner boys to kill Scar."

"That is perfect." She got up from her chair.

"This is exactly what we've been waiting for." He stood with her.

Without thinking, they leaned in and passionately kissed each other. They were both caught up in the excitement of the moment. Dayvid had definitely broken down the barrier that Halleigh had put up.

"So, are we staying here or going to the bedroom?" she asked seductively.

Without saying a word, Dayvid took her by the hand and led her out of the kitchen. Unable to wait until they got to the bedroom, Dayvid had Halleigh up against the hallway wall. They feverishly groped and kissed one another, needing to fulfill their desires.

They slowly made their way down the hall, disrobing each other along the way. Once they made it to the bedroom, Halleigh lay on the bed and Dayvid got on top. They continued kissing and caressing. They rubbed their warm, naked bodies together and explored each other with their tongues and hands. Unlike last time, this time was going to last. They both wanted it to go on forever. This was love; this wasn't just a fuck.

Dayvid slowly kissed his way down Halleigh's body until his head was between her legs. He lovingly kissed and licked and teased her button until she reached an earth-shattering orgasm.

Unable to control her passion and hunger for Dayvid's penis, Halleigh grabbed his head, pulled him up from between her legs, and positioned him to enter her. She grabbed his erect penis and inserted it inside her. He obliged by slowly thrusting in and out of her glistening hole.

Consumed with each other, they were unaware that they were being watched. From the moment they got in the bedroom there had been eyes on them. Detective Derek Fuller was outside the house, looking in.

Derek had met up with the other officer after Day dropped Flex at his apartment. Derek relieved the other officer of his duty and began following Day from that point. Little did he know that if he had just met up with the officer a little earlier, he would have been led directly to Scar. Instead, he'd been following one last dead-end lead and hadn't even bothered to check in with the officer for hours. He'd missed the chance to get to his kids at Scar's safe house.

Instead, when Derek saw Day pull into Halleigh's driveway, he was thinking that maybe this was where his kids were. He parked his car around the corner from the cul de sac and waited until Day went inside. Then he got out and walked around the house, peeking into windows. He was hoping to see his kids in there, but instead, he saw Day in a bedroom with a woman. It looked to Derek like this wasn't just some booty call. The way they were having sex with one another, it looked like they were in love.

Derek watched for a little while, but he didn't want to risk getting caught by either a neighbor or by the love-birds, so he crept back into the woods surrounding the house to wait for Day to leave.

After hours of exploring each other's bodies inside and out, Dayvid and Halleigh lay side by side, exhaust-ed. They were in a state of complete bliss. Both were staring up at the ceiling, trying to catch their breath. They had huge smiles plastered across their faces. Nei-ther one had ever been so satisfied in their lives.

Finally, after several minutes of silence, Dayvid said, "I'm sorry I got you mad at me."

"It was my fault. I overreacted. I should have trusted you," she replied.

"We both overreacted. It's over now. Time to move on."

"Okay. Agreed."

They looked at each other, smiled, and kissed.

"I love you, Hal," Dayvid said.

"I love you too, Dayvid." She kissed him.

They started another round of passionate lovemaking. When it was finished, Dayvid stayed on top of Halleigh. He was propped up on his elbows, face to face with her.

"Everything I do is for you and M.J. I'll always be there for both of you."

"I'll always be there for you. Let's finish our revenge on Scar and Detective Fuller and move on with our life together. Me, you, and M.J.," she said.

"I like that idea." He smiled and kissed her.

"I want to help you kill them. For my own peace."

"I know. I figured." He kissed her forehead.

"How?" she asked.

"I'm not sure yet, but we do it together."

"Like everything from now on." She smiled.

Day got off of Halleigh and sat on the edge of the bed.

"What's wrong?" she asked.

"Nothing. I was just thinking about how happy I am right now." He turned to look at her.

"Me too, baby. Me too."

He got up and started putting on his clothes.

"Where are you going? You're just gonna fuck me and leave me?" she said sarcastically.

"I'm going to finish what I started. Scar's days are numbered. In fact, Scar's hours are numbered."

He leaned over and kissed Halleigh again. She got up and walked him to the front door.

Standing in front of the door, he said, "I love you."

"I love you too. Be careful." She kissed him and hugged him tight.

Halleigh watched from the window as he got into the truck, then she went to the kitchen to prepare a pot of mint tea. She was sitting at the table waiting for the water to boil and thinking about the amazing sex she'd just had when she heard a knock at the door. This put a smile on her face, because she knew it was Day coming back for more. Excited, she got up and went to answer the front door.

"Couldn't get enough?" she asked.

As soon as she opened the door a crack, someone pushed it in and punched Halleigh in her face. The impact knocked her to the ground and knocked her out. Derek walked in and stood over her.

Chapter 16

Collision Course

Mayor Steele walked down the empty corridor of City Hall. It was early morning and he was the first one in the office. This was his daily routine. He would get to work early before anyone else so he could have at least an hour of calm and quiet. He would read the local and national newspapers and catch up on his paperwork. This was always his favorite part of the day, especially lately. Every day seemed to be a replay of the previous day, dealing with chaos and disaster and struggling to keep the city together. There seemed to be daily negative articles about him, and his approval rating was plummeting. Baltimore was on the verge of a revolt, and Mayor Steele was the target. He was stressed out, and it was starting to show in his face. He looked worn down and beaten.

Even though he was struggling, his personality would not let him give up. He was not about to give up his position of power, and would do anything he had to do to keep it.

As he entered his office, he felt that it was going to be a good day. He sat down behind his desk and unloaded his armful of newspapers. Not one paper had a story on the front page about him. This was the first time in a long time that had happened. The mayor felt like maybe things were starting to turn around for him.

With a deep breath in and a heavy sigh, he sat back and opened up the *Baltimore Sun*.

With his morning routine finished, he looked out the window behind his desk, sipping his coffee and watching the commuters arriving to work. When he was feeling good, he loved looking out this window. It reminded him how much he loved the city. On bad days, when he wasn't feeling so good, he hated that window. It reminded him how fickle and heartless his city could be. Today, he loved the city. Even the sun was shining on the plaza in such a way as to say it was going to be a good day. For the first time in a long time, Baltimore seemed to have a feeling of hope in the air.

Later in the day, after several meetings and a press conference, the mayor made his way back to the office with Dexter following.

"Hello, Susan," the mayor greeted.

"Hello, Mayor Steele. Your mail for the day." She handed him a stack of envelopes.

Dexter gave Susan a sleazy wink as he walked by her desk and into the mayor's office. Susan, as usual, ignored him and went about her business.

Dexter and the mayor sat and discussed some political strategy.

"Dexter, I like not having negative headlines about me splashed across the front page of every newspaper. How do we keep this up?"

"Well, sir, I think the worst is behind us. We fended them off long enough that they're getting bored with us. We'll be buried deep within their pages from now on."

"That's not good either. Now we need to get back on the front pages for positive reasons."

"Yes, sir, we do. You're right. I'll talk to our press secretary. Maybe we can do some community outreach and make it a photo op for you." Dexter wrote a few notes on the legal pad on his lap.

"I like that. Start building my image with some pictures of me with some sick kids at a hospital or something." The mayor looked off into the corner of the room, imagining how this photo op would play out.

"Yes, yes. I'll get right on that." Dexter wrote some more notes.

"What's the latest on the thorn in our side, Scar?"

"That hasn't had any changes, sir."

"Damn." The mayor was determined not to lose his good mood.

"But that is good. Nothing worse has happened, so the papers are losing interest." As usual, Dexter stayed optimistic with the mayor.

"Right. I like the positive outlook. I refuse to let this scum ruin my good mood today. Let's start spinning our stories to the press and only accentuate the positive."

"Yes, sir. I like this new you. Anything else?"

As his instinct had told him, the day had gone pretty smoothly for the mayor. It was a slow news day, so to speak. "You know what, Dexter? I'm feeling so good I'm going to give you the rest of the day off."

"Thank you, sir." Dexter smiled and got out while the getting was good.

The mayor started in on his mail. It was the usual—invitations to galas and openings, some magazines, some personal letters. As he flipped through, though, there was one envelope that caught his eye. It was a typical business-size white envelope, but his address was handwritten, and there was no return address. The postmark was from Miami, Florida—another red flag in the mayor's eyes. Being in politics, he knew people in the capital city of Tallahassee, but he knew no one in Miami.

Taking a letter opener out of his desk drawer, he ran it slowly under the flap, making sure not to tip the envelope. After the attacks of 9/11, some news agencies had gotten envelopes with anthrax, and now all government agencies were constantly on high alert for similar attacks. The mayor cautiously opened the letter and looked in for the telltale white powder. When he was satisfied that there was none, he removed the piece of paper inside. He unfolded it and began to read the short, handwritten note:

My condolences to you on the loss of your police chief and chief of staff. I'm coming back for you. You're next!

The mayor got an uneasy feeling in the pit of his stomach. The note confused and troubled him. He hadn't lost either man. In fact, Dexter had just left his office.

He spoke into the intercom on his desk. "Susan, get Chief Hill on the phone."

His uneasiness lessened when he looked out his window and saw Dexter Coram walking across the plaza.

"Sir, Chief Hill is on the line."

"Put him through."

"Hello, Mayor. You must have read my mind. I was just going to call you." Chief Hill sounded upbeat. He was hurriedly gathering his things and preparing to leave his house.

Mayor Steele was relieved when he heard Chief Hill's voice.

"I'm on my way over to police headquarters now. We have solid intel as to the whereabouts of Scar Johnson. We are gathering troops and preparing to raid his house."

"When did this materialize?"

"Late last night, sir. I got a call from one of Scar's associates who goes by the name of Sticks. Apparently they had a falling out, so this kid gave up Scar's location."

On the way to meet Flex, Sticks had called Chief Hill with the information on where to find Scar. Sticks was confident that Flex was getting fed up with Scar's bullshit just as much as he was, so he figured now was the time to take Scar down. He took a preemptive strike and ratted Scar out to the police. Little did he know that Flex was on Scar's side and was about to kill him.

"I knew it was just a matter of time before one of these punks talked," Mayor Steele said.

"The messed up thing is that Scar is hiding in Detective Rodriguez's old house."

"The son of a bitch kills her then hides out in her house? I want this smug fucker taken down!" The mayor pounded his desk.

"It's about to happen." Chief Hill exited his house.

"Chief, you will be front and center at the press conference to announce the capture of this thug."

Chief Hill dropped his duffel bag in the trunk of the car, sat behind the steering wheel, and put the key in the ignition. "Thank you, sir. I promise—" He turned the key.

Boom!

There was a huge blast on the other end of the mayor's phone and then the line went dead.

"Chief Hill! Hello! Chief Hill, are you there? Hello!"
Silence.

"Oh shit." He looked out the window to search for Dexter but didn't see him. He spoke into the intercom. "Susan, get Dexter on the phone."

After a few moments, she responded, "Sir, he's not answering. His phone keeps going straight to voice mail."

"Shit," he repeated.

It turned out not to be a good day.

Dexter was so excited to be off work early that he practically skipped across the plaza. The mayor was in a good mood and being generous, so Dexter was going to take full advantage. Not wanting to be bothered or interrupted, he turned off his cell phone. He was going to have a fun day off. Before leaving City Hall, Dexter had gone to speak to Kris, his intern. He wanted to meet Kris at a hotel.

Kris had been interning for Dexter for about six months. Their relationship started off normally, with Dexter giving Kris menial tasks like making copies, delivering memos, that sort of thing. As the internship progressed, the tasks started becoming more involved, with Dexter even asking Kris's opinion on certain subjects.

One evening, about two months into the internship, Dexter asked Kris to stay a little later to help with a bill that was being presented the next morning. They worked late into the evening, and when they finished, Dexter pulled out a bottle of vodka from his desk and poured drinks for both of them. They sat in Dexter's office drinking vodka.

It was well past midnight when the bottle was finished, and the two were thoroughly drunk. As they were calling it a night and putting on their coats, Dexter grabbed Kris and started kissing him.

Kris had never kissed a man before. He was taken aback; he didn't know what to do. He was confused, drunk, and intimidated. This was his boss kissing him, and he had never thought about sleeping with men before. He pulled away from Dexter, only to have Dexter forcefully grab him back and kiss him again. Dexter then talked Kris into sleeping with him right there in the office.

After several days of awkwardness, Dexter got Kris to sleep with him again. Kris still wasn't fully comfortable with the situation and felt pressured by Dexter, but he thought it would advance his political career, so he did it. Over time, it got easier and easier for Kris, and now they were hooking up on a regular basis.

Dexter couldn't wait to fuck. He was about to get his freak on with this twenty-year-old blond, blue-eyed intern. He had wanted a position of power just so he could use it for things like this. He wasn't a very good-looking guy, so the only way he could get people to sleep with him was to either pay or use his power. Thinking about it on the way to the hotel was getting Dexter hard.

When he arrived at the hotel, he checked in and got the room ready. He opened the mini bar, turned on the music, and positioned the camera. Dexter was into secretly filming his sexual encounters and then watching them later. He had a tiny camera that he aimed at the bed and hid in the closet.

With everything in place, he sat back on the bed and waited. Several minutes later, Kris knocked. Let the games begin. Dexter turned on the camera and answered the door.

Several hours later, after Dexter had done every degrading, kinky thing he could think of, he was preparing to leave the hotel. Kris decided to stay behind and sleep at the hotel. Since it was on Dexter, he was going to order room service and watch some movies.

Turning on his phone, Dexter saw that he had thirty-one voice mails, all seeming to be from the mayor.

"Oh Christ. Party's over," he muttered.

Completely distracted now, he went into the closet, collected his coat, and walked out of the hotel, totally forgetting about his video camera.

Listening to the messages, he walked through the parking garage to his car. They all seemed to say the same thing. It was Susan telling Dexter to call immediately.

Dexter got into his car and dialed the mayor's office, even though he should have been gone for the day. As he listened to the phone ringing on the other end, he turned the key in the ignition and *BOOM!* The car exploded into a fireball of rubber and metal, killing Dexter instantly.

Standing on the street outside of the parking garage, Cecil watched as the car went up in flames on the second level. He took out his phone and placed a call.

"It's done. Both of them are dead."

"Oh, baby. I'm gonna suck your dick so good when you get back down here. I need you. Hurry," Tiphani replied.

She hung up the phone, satisfied that her statement to the mayor was going to be heard loud and clear.

After hearing the explosion over the phone, Mayor Steele instantly went to police headquarters. By the time he arrived, the word was out that Chief Hill had been killed by a car bomb. The headquarters was in a panic. News trucks had already descended on the building, and there were officers buzzing about back and forth. Phones were ringing constantly with news outlets looking for reaction and confirmation.

He entered from the back to avoid the crush of reporters and went directly to the deputy chief's office. There were several people from every rank in the office—sergeants, detectives, lieutenants, all trying to make sense of the tragedy.

An even six feet tall with graying hair and a chocolate complexion, Deputy Chief Vince Worthe was in his early fifties and a lifelong police officer. Although he desperately wanted to be named chief of police, he had been overlooked for the position several times and was resigned to the fact that he would never make chief.

"Mr. Mayor." Vince shook his hand.

"What's the latest? Do we have any leads?"

"We're working on it. Nothing yet, sir."

The mayor handed the note to the deputy chief. "This came to me today."

Vince quickly read the note. He examined the envelope and letter and then handed it to a detective. "Get this to the lab. Fingerprints and DNA."

The detective put it into a clear plastic interdepartmental envelope and left the room, headed toward forensics.

"I was on the phone with him when the bomb exploded. He said you were gathering to raid Scar Johnson's hideout."

"We were just discussing that. We're going to need to speak with you about your conversation with Chief Hill."

"Later. There's no time now. I want this son of a bitch captured. He has terrorized this city for too long."

"We're just about to deploy."

"I want to come with you. I want to see that scum-bag's face when he's captured."

Mayor Steele was swooped up in a sea of officers as they trampled through the underground garage, making their way to vans and squad cars. Someone handed the mayor a bulletproof vest and a windbreaker to wear that read POLICE in big white letters.

Day turned to night on the ride over, and Deputy Chief Worthe filled Mayor Steele in on their plan of attack. They were going to come at him from all angles. Nothing was being left to chance. As far as they were concerned, Scar was armed and dangerous and his men would be looking to kill. The police were taking the same attitude—shoot to kill.

Mayor Steele reinforced the idea that he wanted Scar Johnson kept alive. It would be good for the city's morale if the public saw him in handcuffs. The mayor was not going to allow another bullshit trial. This time Scar would be sentenced to a life in prison.

As they turned the corner onto their destination block, Mayor Steele said, "Deputy Chief, after this is over, I will be promoting you to chief."

"Thank you, sir," he replied; then, into his walkie-talkie he said, "Okay, men. This is it. All units go."

The cars and vans sped up the block and onto the front lawn of Detective Rodriguez's house. The officers jumped out even before some of the vehicles had completely stopped. Some men ran around back. Others ran right up on the front porch with a battering ram and smashed in the front door. All had their guns drawn, ready to shoot.

"Police! Hands up! Police! Get down! Police!" They stormed the house, running from room to room, shouting at the top of their lungs.

The men who entered from the front and the men who entered from the back all converged in the middle of the house. The yelling of "All clear!" slowly died down as all the officers realized that the house was empty. There were signs that people had been there, but no one was there now.

After the commotion subsided, one of the officers called the deputy chief over his handheld radio. "All clear, sir. No sign of anyone. House is empty."

The deputy chief and the mayor walked into the house and surveyed the situation. It was true; the house was empty. It was obvious that whoever had been staying there had left in a hurry.

"Fuck!" the mayor screamed.

Scar got lucky. He didn't know they were planning a raid on his place, but he had heard about the car bombs. He figured that if you were on the police force that day, you were either dealing with the bombing of the police chief or chief of staff Coram's car. They would all be at the crime scenes or dealing with the press. There would be no one setting up or paying attention to roadblocks. Without waiting for another second, Scar gathered up his cash, guns, drugs, and the kids and hightailed it right out of Baltimore. On his way out of town, he drove right past the convoy that was heading to his hideout to bust him.

"Stupid mu'fuckas. Too late. I'm too slick," he muttered and smiled to himself.

Day was on a high. He and Halleigh had finally proclaimed their love for one another. He felt that his life was getting on track. He would have his own piece of the streets, and he would be able to provide for Halleigh and M.J. He was feeling like a real man. In less than an hour he would be rid of Scar, and his new life could start.

They had planned to ambush Scar together, but Day didn't want Halleigh in harm's way, so he decided that he would get it over with as soon as possible. As soon as he left Halleigh's house, he was on his way to kill Scar. To secure his alibi, he made sure to visit a couple of his spots along the way.

Feeling like his alibi would be solid, Day started to hype himself up. He had planned out how he would get Scar to leave the house. He would say that he finally secured a house for them to move into and that they had to move immediately.

He looked at his gun sitting in the seat beside him. Nearing Scar's neighborhood, he picked it up, made sure it was loaded, and cocked it. He wasn't going to take any chances. As he approached the street, Day noticed the block roped off and all kinds of police activity in the area. He put the gun under the seat and drove by the street slowly, craning his neck to see what was happening. As far as he could tell, there were cop cars surrounding Scar's place and officers were walking up and down the neighborhood. Day acted as if he were just passing by and continued on. His destination was directly back to Halleigh.

Just as he left the area, his phone rang.

Derek hog-tied Halleigh while she was knocked out then drove his car into her garage and dumped her in the trunk. He wasn't fucking around anymore. Following Day around seemed to be getting him nowhere closer to finding his kids. Derek was getting the feeling that maybe Day was fucking with him. He wanted to speed the process up, so when he saw Halleigh and Day together, he figured he would kidnap her to get Day to hurry the fuck up. He wanted his kids back, and if they were going to take someone he loved, then he would take someone they loved.

Heading farther out into the countryside, he ended up on an isolated dirt road way out in the woods. It was pitch black, with the only light coming from his headlights and the stars above. Satisfied that he was far away from civilization, Derek stopped his car and got out. He stood at the side of the car for a second to let his eyes adjust to the dark. The one thing that really stuck out to Derek was the stillness and quiet of the country. With eyes adjusted, he walked around to the back of the car and called Day.

"Yo," Day answered. He didn't recognize the number calling.

"You have fun fucking today?"

"Who is this?"

"You know who this is. You have something I love, and now I have something you love."

He opened the trunk. Halleigh was lying in there on her side, bound and gagged. When it opened and the light came on, she started to thrash and scream. It was no use.

"It's your boyfriend Day on the phone," Derek said to her, which caused her to thrash about even more.

Derek removed the gag from her mouth, and she immediately screamed into the phone, "Help me! I'm alone. Help M.J. He's still home. Help—" Derek slammed the trunk shut.

Day's heart sank in his chest. He felt just as helpless as Halleigh sounded. "Motherfucker, you better not touch her," he screamed into the receiver.

"Threats won't work. Just do as I say and nothing will happen to her."

"How much you want?"

"I don't want money, you asshole. I want my kids back."

Day knew then that it was Detective Derek Fuller on the other end of the line.

Derek continued, "Now maybe you'll take me seriously when I say that you need to help me get my kids back. If you don't, you will never see—" He paused. "Funny, I don't even know what your girl's name is. Well, you'll never see her again if you don't do as I say. So, get my kids.

"I will be contacting you soon, and I better like what I hear from you. Stay close to your phone." With that, he ended the conversation.

Day screamed at the top of his lungs and slammed on the accelerator to get to M.J. as fast as he could.

Halleigh had been screaming inside the trunk the whole time. Derek stood outside the trunk, listening to her muffled screams. He pounded on the outside of the trunk and her screaming briefly stopped. After a few seconds, the muffled screams came back. They got louder when Derek finally opened the trunk.

Halleigh's eyes were bloodshot and tears were streaming down her face. Derek reached in to gag her mouth, and Halleigh bit his hand. He screamed in pain and pulled his hand away immediately.

"You bitch." She had bitten him hard enough to draw blood. "I was going to just gag you to shut you the fuck up, but now—" He punched her as hard as he could several times in the face until he was sure she was knocked out. He looked down at her limp, unconscious body and bloodied face.

"You better hope your man comes through or else the inside of this trunk may be the last thing you see." He stuffed the rag back in her mouth and slammed the trunk shut.

He got back into the driver's seat, started the car, and continued driving down the dirt road into darkness. He was on a collision course with Scar and Tiphani, and only one of them would come out alive.

Chapter 17

Comeback

Tiphani raced around her apartment frantically collecting her clothes and throwing them into a suitcase. As soon as she got the phone call from Cecil, she started preparing for her violent return to Baltimore. Her planning phase done, she was now in attack mode. Cecil had done exactly what she had recruited him for, making a deadly first move. Now it was time to dump him.

Yes, he fucked her good, but she could get good dick anywhere. She was done falling under the spell of a man just because he put it on her. Besides, she had come to realize that she was always wanting and curious for new dick. That would never change. Cecil's time was done.

Now she needed to get everything packed and cleaned and out of the house before he got back from Baltimore. It would be easier for everyone involved if she just disappeared. Tiphani had a funny vision of her and Cecil driving on I-95 in opposite directions, she heading north and he heading south, each unaware of the other as they passed.

With the packing finished, Tiphani began to clean the house. She put on dishwashing gloves and wrapped a bandana around her head to keep her hair from falling as she cleaned. She wasn't taking any chances. She was going to erase any trace of herself and clean every inch of the apartment. No hair, no dead skin, no fingerprint would be left behind after she was finished scrubbing. It would be like she was never there. There would be nothing for the cops to tie her to this apartment or to Cecil. She was covering all her tracks.

She went to the cabinet under the kitchen sink and took out her cleaning rags, ammonia, and bleach and started her cleaning frenzy. She was like a tornado whipping through the apartment. Nothing was left untouched in her path. She was scrubbing floors, walls, and ceilings, inside cabinets, drawers, and closets. Furniture was being moved and overturned to clean the underside. There was not an inch of space that was left untouched.

With her first pass through the apartment finished, Tiphani stood in the center of her living room. Day had turned to night. She had been cleaning for hours and hadn't even noticed. The apartment really did look like a tornado had come through. Everything was overturned and out of place. The only way that anyone could tell an actual tornado didn't come barreling through was that everything was sparkling clean.

Keeping on her cleaning attire, Tiphani went into her bedroom to retrieve her suitcase. It was filled so fully she needed to sit on top of it and mash the contents down in order to zip it closed. She dragged the heavy, hulking mass through the living room and set it down at the front door. She was going to make one quick sweep through the apartment, wiping down everything again. When she finished, she planned to be out the front door and on her way to Baltimore to exact revenge on all the hateful men in her life.

She started her quick sweep in the back bathroom and planned to make her way forward until she made it to the front door. On her hands and knees, she was wiping down the tub when she heard the front door open. She remained motionless so as not to make any noise, and slowed her breathing to listen for any sign of who it might be. Her heart pounded in her chest. She wasn't expecting anyone.

A gun would be nice to have right now, she thought.

The door closed and Tiphani heard footsteps coming deeper into the living room. By the softness of the footsteps, she could tell that whoever was there was walking carefully. Tiphani's mind was racing through scenarios of who it might be and how she would escape the situation depending on the person it was.

She was trapped in the back bathroom. There was no window and nothing in there that she could use as a weapon. She thought about hiding in the cabinet under the sink, but quickly realized she wouldn't fit. She thought about trying to sneak out of the bathroom. If she could make it to her bedroom, she could jump out the window, but it was four stories high. It was almost guaranteed that she would break her leg. The hospital was not a place Tiphani wanted to be right now.

Her only option was to go out fighting with her hands. She would wait until they came closer to the bathroom and then be the one to attack first, taking them by surprise and then running out the front door to safety.

The footsteps stopped somewhere in the living room. It was dead silent in the apartment now. Tiphani could feel her heart beating in her chest. A picture of her children flashed across her mind. Was she thinking of them because she was certain this was her end, or was she thinking of them to give her strength to fight? She took it as a sign to fight. She wanted to see her kids again.

She carefully stood up from the kneeling position she had frozen in and quietly positioned herself so she could barge out of the bathroom door and start fighting the intruder. She listened. Still no sounds came from the living room. Tiphani's mind was racing as fast as her heart. Had they left and she didn't hear the door open and close? Was she hearing things? Did someone really enter her apartment?

Then she heard the footsteps slowly and carefully moving again. The intruder took a few steps and stopped again.

"Hello?" a male voice called out.

Tiphani remained silent. The voices in her head and her heartbeat were so loud she was having trouble concentrating on the sound of the voice.

"Hello? Who's there? Anyone?"

She recognized the voice that time. It was Cecil. What was he doing here so soon? He had called her from Baltimore only a few hours ago. Tiphani had to think fast.

"Cecil?" she called out.

"Yeah, it's me."

Tiphani walked guardedly into the living room. "Cecil, what are you doing here?"

"What happened to this place? Did you get robbed? It smells like bleach." Cecil looked around at the overturned furniture.

"No, I didn't get robbed," she said, exasperated. She was annoyed at herself for not moving quicker and getting out of town sooner.

"You planning on going somewhere?" Cecil motioned with his head toward the suitcase at the front door then looked at her with suspicion.

Tiphani was busted. She paused for a brief second before she could come up with something. "Not yet. How did you get home so fast?"

"You aren't happy? You told me to hurry up, so instead of driving back down, I hopped on the next plane. What the hell are you wearing?" He was referring to her bandana and gloves.

"I'm cleaning. This is what I wear when I clean." She acted offended.

"Looks more like you trashed the place. What the fuck is going on here?"

"I told you I'm cleaning."

"Cut the bullshit! Tell me what is fucking going on. I just came back from handling your business, and it look to me like you're trashing the place and getting ready to leave. Without me!" He took a threatening step toward Tiphani.

"Baby. What?" Tiphani used a cooing tone to try to soothe Cecil. "Yes, I'm getting ready to leave, but not without you. I was so excited when you called that I went in motion and started to get everything in order to leave as soon as you came back." She took a sensual step toward him.

"Why your bag look like you ready to leave right now?" Cecil wasn't that easily swayed.

"Like I said, I got excited. I got excited because you had sent the message to the mayor and because I knew you would be coming back . . ." She pressed her tits against Cecil and grabbed his ass then continued. ". . . and I could suck your dick again."

Cecil pushed her off of him. "Why does it smell like bleach? What the fuck you trying to clean that much? Did you kill someone?"

Tiphani laughed at that. "No, I didn't kill anyone." She didn't have any good excuse for cleaning with bleach and didn't see the point in lying about it, so she told him the truth. Well, sort of.

"I was making sure to get rid of any trace of either one of us ever being here. My bag was at the door because I was going to put it in the car and wait for you and stop you before you entered the apartment so you wouldn't track any of your DNA in here. Then we could head back up to Baltimore together."

Cecil took a second to absorb everything she said. It sounded convincing and seemed like it might be true. He wanted to believe her. She was fine as hell and fucked like no one he had ever met before. Plus, she had enough money for both of them to live off of for the rest of their lives.

Fuck it. It might be true, he thought.

"There's one problem with your idea," Cecil said.

"What?" Tiphani was afraid that he didn't believe her.

"When were you going to suck my dick like you promised?" Cecil smiled a devilish grin.

Tiphani smiled too because she was so relieved that he had believed her story. She got down on her knees, unbuckled his pants, and pulled out his dick. She sucked him off and swallowed every ounce of his semen when he came.

"Damn, baby, that shit felt good." Cecil buttoned his pants as Tiphani picked herself up of the floor.

"Well, you taste good, baby." Tiphani wiped her mouth and licked her fingers. "I'm going to take my suitcase to the car. Then I'll come back and do one last quick wipe-down of the apartment."

"No. I'll take it to the car. You stay and clean and then come out. I don't want to get the apartment any dirtier. That is why you swallowed my jizz, isn't it?" Cecil smiled as he grabbed the suitcase and went to the car.

He wasn't about to let her leave before him. He had a feeling that if he hadn't come home when he did, she would have been ghost and he would have never seen her again. He was not about to let her out of his sight right now. Cecil wanted that money of Tiphani's and was going to make sure he got a piece of it.

Damn. I'm not going to be able to ditch him, Tiphani thought. *I guess he's coming to Baltimore with me.*

Tiphani finished wiping down the apartment and went out to the car. Cecil was sitting in the driver's seat, waiting for her. She got in the passenger's side, buckled her seatbelt, and said,

"Here I come, Baltimore. You better be ready for my comeback. Let's go get me some revenge."

Cecil put his foot on the accelerator and sped off, heading north. Destination: Baltimore.

Chapter 18

Won't Back Down

Scar drove up the winding dirt driveway in the sub-urban hills north of Baltimore. His destination was a secluded farmhouse surrounded by one hundred acres of forest. He reached over and pulled one of his guns out of the glove compartment, laying it in his lap as his niece and nephew slept in the backseat. His GPS told him this was his destination, but that meant nothing to Scar. His trust of technology was the same as his trust in people, which was to say it was zero. If there happened to be anyone occupying this house and they saw him, he would have to blast them to protect his identity.

He rolled around the last bend and came upon the white-shingled two-story house. The headlights of his car searched over the house and revealed its empti-ness. Scar relaxed a little, seeing it was the right house. He stopped the car then roused the kids and hustled them up the walkway and into their new bedroom on the second floor, where they fell right back to sleep.

Scar walked around the house after unpacking the car. He inspected every room, opening all closet doors and cabinets. This was his new safe house, and he want-ed to know every inch of it. It was pretty bare bones right now. The only things occupying the place were beds for him and the kids. Until he had seen the place with his own eyes and could assess the situation, he didn't want to draw any attention by moving in a bunch of stuff and having a lot of traffic in and out. Now that he was there, he saw how secluded it was and decided there was nothing to worry about. Now he needed his shit and he needed it fast. He hated when his houses would produce echoes because there was nothing in them to absorb the sound. Wanting to get the ball rolling on filling the house, Scar called Flex.

"Ay yo," Flex answered.

"Where the fuck you at?"

"On my way, boss. These country roads be fucked up. I got all turned around, but I'm on the right track now."

"You take care of your problem?" Scar asked.

"That stick been snapped in two. Broken beyond repair and buried back where it came from." Flex was proud to be able to give Scar the good news.

"Your wallet better be stuffed."

"Overflowing, boss. You ain't got to worry 'bout me. I'ma always do you right," Flex boasted.

"Good lookin', nigga. You just moved up the ladder, soldier."

"I like the sound of that."

"We gotta fill this place. There ain't shit here. Any word from Day?" Scar looked around the empty dining room.

"Nah."

"A'ight. This nigga better not be locked up. He ain't answer when I call him." He had called Day while Day was on the phone with Derek. Day wasn't about to answer the other line while he was trying to deal for Halleigh's life, so he ignored Scar's call.

Scar looked in the refrigerator for the second time, knowing damn well that it would still be empty. "I need some food, nigga. Stop off and get something for me."

"I got you."

Scar ended the call as he walked into the empty living room. He stood in front of the bay window that overlooked the tree-covered valley below. The valley started filling with light as the sun peeked over the horizon.

Scar felt a million miles from Baltimore. He needed the energy of the city. This country life was bullshit. He hated it. He had only been there for an hour, and he was already getting stir crazy.

There was no way he would be able to stay here long. He felt like he wouldn't have as much control over his operation. He was out of sight while undercover in Baltimore, but at least he was in the city and his soldiers knew it. With him being so far away, there was no guarantee that they would follow his orders. This was going to test Scar and his control over his crew.

Fuck this. This ain't right. He made a call.

"This is Fuller. Go." Derek answered his cell phone as he drove down the deserted country road.

"What's good, brother?" Scar continued looking out the window as the wildlife started to awaken to a new day.

Derek's heart sank for a second. He was caught off guard. He wasn't expecting to hear this voice on the other end of the phone.

Neither man said a word. The only sound each could hear was the other one breathing into the receiver. Their emotions were all over the place. It had been a while since they had heard each other's voices. As much as they hated one another, their family bond was making it difficult to know how to proceed with the conversation.

"How'd you get this number?" Derek asked.

"Day gave you that phone. Who the fuck you think paid for it? Think, nigga," Scar explained like he was talking to a five-year-old.

"Don't talk down to me, mu'fucka."

"Chill, nigga."

"Fuck you." Derek couldn't hide his contempt for his brother. The tone for this conversation had now been set. This wasn't going to be a friendly chat.

Derek continued, "Give me my kids."

Scar smiled to himself. Instantly he knew he still had the upper hand on his brother. "What? No 'how are you, how you been'?"

"Fuck your sarcasm. I'm coming for you, and not one hair on my kids' heads better be out of place."

"Your kids are fine, and if you play along, you won't have nothing to worry about, so back up off that 'coming for you' bullshit," Scar warned.

"I'm working on getting the mayor's help." Derek realized he didn't have much to bargain with, so he backed off the threats.

"I ain't talking about that. I don't need that mu'fucka's help no more. I put Baltimore in my rearview. What I'm talking about is you and me working together like old times. Everybody wins."

"I'm not officially on the force anymore."

"But you still got connections, and we could make it so you get cleared of all charges."

"I don't need your help, and I damn sure ain't helping you. You best just get me my kids, mu'fucka." Derek forgot that Scar held all the cards and that he needed to be diplomatic in his approach.

"You makin' a mistake, brother."

"Don't call me brother. We ain't family no more. A brother would never do what you did. Family stays loyal to one another."

This hit Scar in the heart. Derek was right; he hadn't been a good brother. Was he sorry for his actions toward his brother? Yes, but there was no turning back the clock now.

"Look, what's done is done. You should think about the present and look toward the future."

"I am looking toward the future. I'm gonna continue coming for you, and I'm gonna be reunited with my kids. I won't back down."

Derek had enough of the conversation and ended the call. He had leverage on Day and would use it to find Scar and keep his kids alive, so he saw no reason to deal with Scar and his negotiations. He would find his deceitful brother and end his life.

Scar heard the silence on the other end of the phone line and returned the phone to his pocket. The sun was now completely over the horizon, and a new day was born as Scar came to the realization that the relationship with his brother was dead.

Flex entered the house with some fast food hamburgers. He handed a bag to Scar, and they both sat on the floor. Scar ate in silence as his thoughts drifted to his brother and the fact that he was going to have to be the one to kill him once and for all.

Chapter 19

From Bad to Worse

The day after Dexter and Chief Hill were killed, Mayor Steele sat slumped over his desk with his forehead resting on the desktop. He was exhausted and emotionally spent. The previous twenty-four hours had gone from being great to a complete disaster, with his emotions going up and down like a yo-yo the whole time. Now he had the task of leading the investigation into who was responsible for the bombings, keeping his city calm, and planning the funerals of two of his most trusted aides.

The door to his office opened, causing the mayor to lift his head. He had no idea how long he had been slumped over. If he had it his way, he would have stayed like that all day.

"Hello, Susan." He wiped his mouth and smoothed his hair.

"Hello, Mr. Mayor," replied his trusty secretary.

"What can I do for you?"

"Your mail, sir." She placed a bundle of envelopes on his desk.

"Thank you, dear." The mayor reached for the bundle.

"You look awful, sir. Is there anything I can do?"

"You're very kind, Susan. Thank you." He gave a half-hearted smile.

"I just want to say I'm sorry. No matter my personal feelings toward someone, I would never wish death on them." She was sincere. Dexter was disgusting and creepy, but she thought death was undeserved even for him.

The mayor thanked her again then dismissed her. As she approached the door, two armed state troopers came storming in, practically knocking her to the floor. Following right behind them came the governor of Maryland, Thomas Tillingham.

At five feet four inches, Governor Tillingham was dwarfed by the two burly guards as he strode into the room. He had the swagger and attitude of a man trying to compensate for his lack of height. He was popular with the citizens of Maryland, but in political circles, he was not well liked. His rise to the governorship was contemptuous, with many people being taken advantage of and lied to every step of the way. Like so many politicians, he got into public office with the best of intentions, but when he saw how the game worked behind closed doors, with all the deals, false promises, and backstabbing going on, he quickly changed his tune. He realized he'd better start looking out for himself or he wouldn't be in politics for very long. Thus began his career as a ruthless politician who was willing to do anything to anyone who opposed him.

"Excuse you," Susan said to the state troopers then turned to the mayor. "Shall I stay, Mr. Mayor? Do you need me to call anyone?"

"No, Susan. I'm fine."

Susan composed herself and walked out of the room, glaring at the rude state troopers, who just ignored her.

"Close the door, Henry," the governor instructed the bigger of the two officers as he stood in front of Mayor Steele's desk. The two politicians faced off, looking each other in the eye. It was like an old Western show-down between two cowboys, each waiting for the other to draw first. There was no love lost between these two men.

Governor Tillingham was halfway through his term and had enjoyed a high approval rating with the people of his state, but lately that rating had begun to slip and he blamed it on the mess happening in Baltimore. Most of their contact was over the phone, but Governor Tillingham thought it was time to meet face to face. He worked hard to create his image and amass his power, and he was not about to let the mismanagement of Baltimore ruin that.

"Mathias." Not breaking eye contact, the governor nodded his head slightly in a gesture of greeting.

"Thomas." The mayor mirrored the governor's movements.

Both men stayed standing. Each wanted to assume the position of power, and standing was a more powerful position. In their minds, the first to sit was weaker.

"Let me begin by saying I'm sorry for the loss of two fine men," the governor said.

"They were two of the finest and loved their city as much as anyone." The thought of his two men made the mayor forgot about his mind games with the governor. With his mind elsewhere, he sat in his chair. The governor followed his lead and did the same. Now it was time to get to serious business.

"Now let me say, what the fuck is going on in this city?" The governor's tone made his anger apparent.

"We have it under control," the mayor responded with a flippant tone.

"It's that attitude that got you into this mess and the reason I had to come down here."

"What do you mean 'that attitude'?" Mayor Steele squinted his eyes at the governor.

"Like maybe you aren't taking this seriously enough."

"Two of my staff were murdered. You don't think I'm taking that seriously? You don't think I'm doing everything in my power to find whoever did this?"

"See, there's the problem. I'm not sure how much power you actually have left. Is anyone taking you seriously anymore? Your city is falling apart, crime is running rampant, and now city officials are being murdered. In fact, this isn't the first police chief to be murdered while you were in office. Have you found the person responsible for that one yet? Seems to me that the criminals in this city have no fear or respect for you. At this point, how can you expect any part of your police force or government to have faith in any of your decisions?"

"With all due respect, fuck you. I have not lost anyone's respect. I've probably gained more of it. I rode along when we went to apprehend Scar Johnson. My police force has been working so hard we found where that bastard was hiding." The Mayor did not like getting disrespected in his own office.

"So, where is he, Mathias? Is he in custody? Why isn't it front page news?" The governor's words were dripping with sarcasm.

"He cleared out before we got there."

"One step behind, as usual." The Governor smirked and raised his eyebrows.

"Get out! Get out of my office now! I am sick of your disrespect." The mayor shot up from his chair. He was now looking down on Governor Tillingham.

If there was one thing that would set off Thomas Tillingham, it was when someone hovered over him as a form of intimidation. Growing up, he was always the smallest one in the room, so he used it as motivation. It pissed him off if someone thought him to be inferior because of his height, and he would go to great lengths to prove them wrong and embarrass them in the process. This attempt by Mathias Steele to intimidate him was about to backfire.

"Who in God's name do you think you are speaking to?" He slowly rose from his seat. "You have fucked this city up since the day you started. Your whole time in office has been marked with corruption, greed, and murder, and I, for one, am sick of it. These last two murders are the final straw. I came down here today to give you the opportunity to step down, but now seeing your attitude, I am prepared to start impeachment proceedings." He was staring daggers into Mayor Steele.

The mayor was stunned. He stood with his mouth open for a few seconds before he spoke. "You're what? You can't do that."

"I can, and I will."

"Please, Thomas, you can't. It'll ruin me."

"That's exactly the point. You'll be finished." The governor shrugged his shoulders matter-of-factly.

Mayor Steele's voice rose an octave. "Let's talk about this, please."

"There's nothing left to talk about. I've said all I have to say."

"What can I do to change your mind? Give me a chance. I promise I'll catch Scar and bring him to justice. I'll give you the credit for it if you want."

"You can't change my mind. My approval ratings have dropped ever since this shit storm started here in Baltimore. It's time for that to change—starting with getting rid of you. As far as credit is concerned, I will get credit for capturing Scar, because I am personally going to take over the case. That piece of garbage won't be polluting my state much longer."

"I'll fight it. I'll fight it and win. You can't bully me."
The mayor came out from behind his desk.

"Go ahead, but I don't recommend it. You'll spend
millions in legal fees, and you'll still end up losing.
You'll look even worse after it's all said and done. But if
you choose to fight it, I look forward to crushing you in
court and in public."

Governor Tillingham was right. It would cost millions that the mayor didn't have. It would be a useless
fight. The only option he had was to try to salvage his
job, and if not that, then maybe he could just convince
the governor to let him step down with some dignity.

"I'll pay you. How much do you want? At least let me
resign on my own terms." The mayor's begging was out
of control. He actually went down to his knees.

"Stop embarrassing yourself." The governor shook
his head in disgust and walked out of the office with the
two burly state troopers on his heels.

Mayor Steele stayed frozen on his knees. His whole
world had just come crashing down on him. His political career was over. The position he worked so hard to
attain was now going to be taken from him instantly.
Not only would he never be a politician again, but no
one would want to hire him. He would be considered
toxic in the business world. Having a disgraced mayor
on the payroll would hurt the bottom line, and if that
caused them to lose money, then it wasn't going to happen. He would be unemployed and broke.

Mayor Steele stayed in the same position for several
minutes. He was in a state of mild shock. He couldn't
move even if he wanted to. He was so overwhelmed
with what just occurred that his mind went empty for
a little while, just so he could cope with the severity of
his situation.

When he snapped out of his trance, he noticed there were tears running down his cheeks. He wiped his cheeks dry with the palms of his hands and stood up. He looked around at his office, hoping that something might give him a sign as to what he should do next. No signs jumped out at him.

He slowly walked on weak knees to his desk chair. If he had a gun, he would have shot himself right then and there. He sat at his desk, looking at his office, thinking about his situation. Scar Johnson had imposed his will on the city of Baltimore, and the mayor had done everything he could to try to stop him. This wasn't the mayor's fault; this was Scar Johnson's fault. The mayor's life was over because of one man, and that was Scar Johnson.

The mayor thought longer about his situation and blamed Derek and Tiphani Fuller as well. If Derek had found Scar like he said he would, then the mayor could have arrested him. If Tiphani wasn't such a ho and hadn't fucked Scar then helped him get acquitted, none of this would have happened.

The mayor wanted blood. If he was going down, he was bringing them down with him. He was going to get revenge on all of them, starting with Scar. He would find and kill him personally; then Tiphani and Derek would be next to die.

His mood suddenly perked up now that he sort of had a plan. He opened his briefcase and started stuffing in as many of his files as he could. When he was finished, he took one last look around his office. This was going to be his last time there. He wasn't planning on coming back. He was done being mayor of the city of Baltimore.

Fuck this ungrateful city, he thought. He had a mind to torch the office, but thought better of it.

He walked into the waiting room where Susan was sitting. She had been there since the governor had barged in. After the guard closed the door, Susan put her ear to the door and heard every word that was said between the governor and the mayor. The look in the mayor's eyes scared Susan. She was speechless as he spoke to her.

"Susan, I want to thank you for your years of loyal service to me. Take care of yourself and enjoy the rest of your life." The mayor shook her hand and walked out the door and into the next chapter of his life. He was now a civilian with nothing to lose, looking to kill for revenge.

Susan sat alone at her desk, not sure of what to do. She felt she had just seen the mayor for the last time. There was a bad feeling in her soul that a storm was brewing in Baltimore, and it was going to be violent.

Exerpt

A GIRL FROM FLINT

Prologue

Karma is what put me in that hellhole. I don't even know how I ended up in jail. A couple years ago I was on top of the world. I've had more money flow through my hands than most people ever see in their entire lives. I was the woman that everybody wanted, and I had my way with some of the richest men in the Midwest. From prestigious businessmen to the most hood-rich niggas in Flint, I've had them all. We thought it was a game, and in a way it was. We were trained to be the best. Skilled in the art of seduction, we were professionals who knew how to please in every sexual way. In my family the mentality was, if you ain't fucking, you don't eat.

Growing up in the hood, I had to use what I had to get what I wanted. My pussy was my meal ticket, and in order to stay on top, I juiced every nigga green to the game. I felt like, if a dude was stupid enough to let me trick him out of his dough, then he deserved to get got. "Fuck me, pay me" was our motto, and I used to laugh when my girls used to shout that after we hustled men out of their money.

It's not quite as funny these days though. Now I've got a prison sentence hanging over my head, and I'm locked in this cage like an animal. I haven't washed my hair in months, and I'm looking over my shoulder every minute of every day, hoping these bitches in here won't try to get at me. I don't know, maybe it was my destiny. All the wrong that I've done, all that shit came back like a boomerang and hit me harder than I could have ever imagined. I sit in this jail cell every day wondering how I landed in a state prison, a maximum-security state prison at that.

When I heard the judge say those words, it brought tears to my eyes. It was like a nightmare and I was dreaming about my worst fear. Only, I couldn't wake up. It was real, and there was no waking up from it.

My downfall was . . . well, you'll learn about that later.

From the very beginning of my life, I was headed in a downward spiral. My mother is a crack fiend, and I haven't seen or spoken to her in years. I never knew my father. He died before I got the chance to get to know him. I hear that he really loved me, but the fact that he wasn't in my life affected me. I never had that male figure in my life, and that pains me greatly.

As you read this novel, understand that this is what happened to me, and that everything that you do has its consequences. I remember we would talk about opening up our own salon and not needing a nigga to support us. That was before my life got complicated. Believe me, if I could turn back the hands of time, I would have never stepped foot in the murder capital—Flint, Michigan.

Yeah, that was the first of our mistakes. Honey made it seem so live, so wonderful. I thought it was the city that would make all my dreams come true. The truth of the matter is, everyone in that damn city has hidden agendas and is looking for a way to get paid, by any means necessary. I was a little girl trying to do big things in a small city. I should've just kept my ass in good ol' New York.

Me and my girls thought we were the shit. We got whatever we wanted, when we wanted it; from dick to pocketbooks, even first-class vacations around the world. We used men until their pockets ran out, and when we were done, we tossed them aside and moved along to the next. Some people may call us hoes, gold-diggers, or even high-paid prostitutes, but nah, it wasn't like that. It was our hustle, and trust me, it paid well. Very well.

I wish I could go back to the good ol' days when we used to smoke weed in Amra's room and open the windows so Ms. Pat wouldn't find out. Or the days when we used to lie about staying the night over each other's house so we could go to parties and stay out all night. Those are the memories that make this place bearable. Those are the times that I reflect on when I get depressed and when life seems unfair. The times when it was just me, Honey, Amra, and Mimi, the original Manolo Mamis.

There have been many after us, but none like us. All them other bitches are just watered-down versions of what we used to be. That's who we were, that was our clique. That's the friendship that I miss, and think about when I feel lonely. The thought of how close we used to be is something I would cherish forever.

I know I'm rambling on and on about me and my girlfriends. You are probably wondering, *Bitch, how did you end up in jail?*

Damn, I'm so busy trying to tell y'all what happened, I forgot to introduce myself. I know y'all wanna read about Sunshine and Shai and all that high-school bullshit, but let me get my piece off first. I promise you, you won't be disappointed. I'm Tasha, and this is my Flint story.

Chapter One

1994

As Lisa looked into the mirror, she could not recognize the eyes that stared back at her. Everything started running through her mind all at once. She thought about the loss of her only love Ray, his death, and about their creation, Tasha. Tasha was the only positive thing in her life. Her bloodshot eyes stared into the mirror as she looked into her lifeless soul and began to cry.

Lisa tied a leather brown belt around her arm and began to slap her inner arm with two fingers, desperately searching for a vein. As the tears of guilt streamed down her face, she looked at the heroin-filled needle on the sink and reached for it. She hated that she had this terrible habit, but it called for her. She wasn't shooting up to get high anymore, she was doing it to feel better. She needed the drug. She tried to resist it, but the drug called out to her more and more. When she wasn't high, she was sick and in tremendous pain, and her body fiended for it.

She injected the dope into her vein and a warm sensation traveled up her arm. The tears seemed to stop instantly, and her frail body slowly slumped to the floor, her eyes staring up into space. All of Lisa's emotions and her negative thoughts slowly escaped her mind as she began to smirk. She could not shake this habit that a former boyfriend had introduced her to, and her weekend binges eventually became an addiction.

Her addiction affected her life, as well as her daughter's. All of her welfare checks sponsored the local dope man's chrome rims, ice, and pocket money. Her life started going downhill after the death of Raymond Parks, better known as Ray.

It was 1982, the era of pimping. Lisa was fifteen when she met Ray, who was twenty-one at the time and a known pimp in the area. Ray approached Lisa while she was walking to the store. He pulled up and slyly said, "Hey, sweetness. Wanna ride?"

Lisa paid him no mind and kept walking. She started switching her ass a little harder while walking, knowing she had an audience. She pretended not to be flattered by the older man and flipped her blond, sandy-brown hair.

Ray parked his long Cadillac at the corner and stepped his shiny gators onto the streets of Queens. He took his time and eventually caught up with the thick young woman with hazel eyes. He slid in front of Lisa, blocking her path. "Hello, beautiful. My name is Raymond, but my friends call me Ray. I wouldn't have forgiven myself if I didn't take the time out to meet you." Ray stuck out his hand and offered a handshake.

Lisa looked up and saw a tall, lean, brown-skinned young man. She couldn't stop her lips from spreading, and she unleashed her pretty smile. She shook his hand and said with a shaky voice, "I'm Lisa."

Raymond smiled and stared into her eyes. Lisa stared back, and her eyes couldn't seem to leave his. He knew he had her when he saw that all too familiar look in her eyes. He asked in a smooth, calm voice, "Can I take you out sometime?"

"My mama might not like that."

Ray smiled. "Just let me handle her. So, can I take you out sometime or what?"

Lisa blushed. "Yeah, I guess that'll be all right."

Raymond gave her his number and asked her how old she was. Lisa told him that she was only fifteen. Ray's facial expression dropped, disappointed to know she was so young. He didn't usually approach girls her age, but she had an adult body and was by far the most beautiful girl he'd ever seen. He grabbed her hand, looked at her, and told her to give him a call so he could pick her up later that day.

Lisa watched Ray get into his car and pull off. She couldn't stop smiling to herself as she continued to walk to the store. *He was a fly brother. I hope my momma let me go.* She hurried to the store so she could get home and call Ray. She knew that it would take a miracle for her to get her mother's approval, but as fine as Ray was, she was definitely going to try.

Lisa called Ray later that evening, and an hour later he was at her front door with a dozen roses in each hand.

Lisa's mother answered the door and was impressed by the well-dressed young man that stood before her. She noticed he wasn't around Lisa's age and became skeptical about letting him in.

Ray sensed the vibe and quickly worked his magic. He handed the flowers to her and took off his hat to show respect.

Ray didn't get to take Lisa out that night. He and Lisa's mother talked, and he charmed her for hours. He barely spoke to Lisa the entire evening. A professional at sweet-talking, he knew that to get Lisa, he had to get her mother first.

As the night came to an end, Ray said good-bye to Lisa's mother and asked if Lisa could walk him to his car. She agreed, and they exited the house.

Lisa and Ray stood in the driveway. He took her by the hand and said, "I never saw a lady so fly. I want you to be mine . . . eventually. What school do you go to?"

"McKinley."

Ray shook his head then said in a soft voice, "I know where that's at. I'll pick you up after school tomorrow, okay?"

Lisa started to cheese. "Really?"

He grabbed Lisa's head, kissed her forehead softly, and whispered, "See you tomorrow."

She turned around and entered her mother's house, and Ray took off as soon as he saw that she got in safely.

The next day Ray was parked outside of the high school in his Cadillac waiting for his new "pretty young thang," as he called her.

When she got into the car, Ray smiled at her. "Hello, beautiful. How was your day?"

From that day on, Ray and Lisa were together. He took her on shopping sprees weekly, and she was happy with her man. He never asked for sex and never rushed or pressured her in any way. Lisa wondered why the subject never came up and wondered if he was physically attracted to her.

Ray was very much attracted to her, but he'd promised himself he wouldn't touch her until she was eighteen. He had his hoes and women all over town, so sex was never an issue.

Lisa knew about his other women and his line of work but never complained. Ray took care of her and treated her like a queen at all times. Over time she fell deeply in love with him and never had a desire to mess with any other man.

Ray always made sure she had whatever she wanted and that she went to school everyday. If she didn't do well in school, her gifts would stop, so Lisa became a very good student.

Occasionally Ray would help Lisa's mother with bills and put food in their refrigerator. Ray had money, real money. He was a pimp with hoes all over the city. He wasn't the type to put his hands on a woman. He made exceptions for the hoes that played with his chips or disrespected him. But, in general, he had mind control over many women, so violence was rarely needed.

Exactly one month after her eighteenth birthday, Lisa found out she was pregnant with Ray's child. She couldn't believe she had gotten knocked up on her first time, but when she told Ray, he was the happiest man on earth. Lisa dropped out of school, and Ray immediately moved her from her mother's house and into his plush home in the suburbs.

He used to put his head on Lisa's stomach every night and tended to her every need. He promised that when he saved up enough money, he would open a business and exit the pimping game.

Eight months into her pregnancy, Lisa began to become jealous of Ray and all his women and confronted him about it.

Ray reacted in a way that Lisa never saw. He raised his voice and said, "Don't worry about me and my business! You just have my baby girl and stand by yo' man!" He stormed out the house and slammed the front door.

Lisa felt bad for confronting him and began to cry. She cried for hours because she'd upset the only man she ever loved. Ray was all she knew. She stayed up and waited for his return, but he never came.

That night Ray went around town to collect his money from his workers. He was upset with himself for raising his voice at Lisa. He'd never yelled at her before, so it was really bothering him.

He pulled his Cadillac onto York Avenue and saw one of his best workers talking with a heavyset man about to turn a trick. He thought to himself, *Make that cheddar, Candy.* He decided to wait until Candy finished her business before collecting from her. He sat back in his seat and turned the ignition off, sat back and listened to the smooth sounds of the Isley Brothers and slowly rocked his head.

He looked back at Candy and noticed that the man and Candy were entering a car parked on the opposite side of the street. Candy was his "bottom bitch." She always kept cash flowing and never took days off. He smiled. *Candy going to make that fool cum in thirty seconds.*

Suddenly he saw Candy jump out the car, spitting and screaming at the man. She walked toward the sidewalk spitting. The man jumped out the car and started to yell at Candy, and yelled even louder when Candy kept on walking.

At this point Ray calmly stepped out the car and began to head toward her. The man had gotten to Candy and began to grab her and was screaming at the top of his lungs. Ray approached the man from behind and grabbed him. "Relax, relax."

"Mind yo fucking business, playa. This bitch is trying to juke me out of my money."

"Daddy Ray, he pissed in my mouth! He didn't say shit about pissing. I don't get down like that."

Before Ray could say anything, the man lunged at Candy, slamming her head hard into the brick wall she was leaning on. Ray immediately grabbed the man by the neck and began to choke him. His fingers wrapped tightly around his neck, Ray whispered to him, "Never put your hands on my hoes. If I see you around here again, it's you and me, youngblood." Ray released the man, and he dropped to the ground, trying to catch his breath. Ray stood over the man and pulled out a money clip full of cash. "How much did you give her?"

"Forty. I gave her forty," the man said, rubbing his neck.

Ray peeled off two twenties and threw it at the man and told him to get the fuck out of his office. The man took the money and ran to his car and pulled off.

Ray then turned around to help Candy up. She was lying motionless. He quickly bent down to aid her and noticed she wasn't breathing. He started to shake her and call her name, "Candy! Candy!" He got no response.

He gave her mouth-to-mouth resuscitation, and she began to breathe lightly. He knew he had to get her to the hospital, but he didn't want to be the one to take her in. It would raise suspicion if a known pimp brought a half-dressed hooker in, barely breathing and battered. He decided to go in her purse to see if he could find a number for someone that she knew, to check her into the hospital.

As soon as he stuck his hand in her purse, he saw flashing lights and heard a man on a bullhorn telling him to put his hands up. Then another police car pulled up.

Ray stood up, both of his hands in the air.

One of the police officers ran to the girl and put his fingers on her neck. He shook his head. The policemen handcuffed Ray and began to read him his rights.

"Wait, man, you got this all wrong—"

"Yeah, yeah." The cop led Ray to this police car.

Ray began to pull away from him. "Listen, I was helping her. I didn't—"

Another cop hit Ray over the head with a billy club. "You got caught red-handed robbing this young lady. People like you make me sick."

Ray was too dazed to say anything as the cops put him in the back of the police car. He knew it looked bad for him. He dropped his head and began to pray.

The prosecutor stood up to give his closing argument. He wiped his forehead with a handkerchief then slowly approached the jury. "The man sitting in that defendant chair is a man of no remorse. He killed a seventeen-year-old girl in cold blood. Imagine if that girl was your daughter, your sister, or a beloved neighborhood child." He paused for effect. He wanted to give the jury time to process the information what he'd just said. He pointed his finger at Ray. "This man is a menace to society and deserves to be punished to the fullest extent of the law. All of the evidence points toward one man. And that man is sitting before us today. That man is Raymond Parks. Nothing can keep our communities safe from this tyrant except a life sentence. The only people who can make that happen are you, the people of the jury. Don't put another young girl in danger. Put him away for the rest of his life. He was caught over his victim's dead body rummaging through her purse looking for money. He drove this woman's skull against a

brick wall so hard and so violently, her brain hemor-
rhaged, which ultimately led to her death. How cold-
blooded is that? So the prosecution asks of you—no, we
beg of you—the jury to sentence this man to a lifetime
in prison. Render a guilty verdict and bring justice back
to the community. I rest my case." The prosecuting attorney turned and walked back to his seat, a smug grin
on his face. He knew he'd just delivered a closing argument that would cripple the defense and win the trial.

Ray looked back at Lisa and her swollen belly and
felt an agonizing pain in his heart. He might spend the
rest of his life in jail for a crime he didn't commit. He
felt tears well up in his eyes as he mouthed the words,
"I love you," to Lisa.

Lisa looked into Ray's eyes and began to cry. She
knew that the chances were slim for him to get off. She
gripped the bench she was sitting on. *Please God let
them find him not guilty. Please . . . I need him,* she
prayed as the jury deliberated in a private room.

Half an hour later, the jury returned to the courtroom with the verdict. An overweight old white man
stood up and looked into Raymond's eyes and said,
"We, the jury, find the defendant Raymond J. Parks
guilty of murder in the second degree and guilty of
strong-armed robbery."

Lisa screamed when the verdict was pronounced.

Ray dropped his head as the guards came over to
escort him out of the courtroom. He looked at his attorney. "That's it? You said you could beat this case.
I'm innocent, man. I'm innocent."

His attorney looked at him, shrugged his shoulder,
and gave a sly smile. "We'll file an appeal."

Ray knew that his chances of winning the appeal
would be just as slim as his chances of winning the
trial. He looked at Lisa as they carried him out the

courtroom. "I love you," he mouthed again as the guards handcuffed him.

Lisa felt so much pain in her heart. She just stood there and watched her only love leave her life. Helpless, she didn't know what to do. Ray was going to prison, and there was nothing she could do to stop it from happening.

She was so distraught, she couldn't control herself. She felt her dress become soaked and thought she had peed on herself. She felt liquid run down her leg and then realized it wasn't urine. Her water had broken. "I'm going into labor," she screamed to Ray just as the guards took him from her sight.

Her mother told her to sit down and then called a guard over for help.

Later that evening, Tasha Parks was born. It was the worst day of Lisa's life. The love of her life had been convicted of murder, and ironically their child was born on the same day.

Lisa was depressed for months and cried herself to sleep every night with her newborn baby in her arms.

Ray left behind a house and some money in the bank, so she supported herself and her daughter with that.

Lisa visited Ray as soon as they let her. He had grown a beard and walked to the table where a thick glass window separated them. She picked up the phone, and so did Ray. Ray did not have the same look in his eye that he used to have. The sparkle had diminished. Lisa desperately looked, trying to find a piece of the man she had fallen in love with, but it wasn't there. He had changed. There was no warm feeling in his eyes anymore, only coldness.

"How are you?" she asked, trying to be supportive.

Ray shook his head and smiled. "Don't worry about me. Just make sure you take care of our child. Lisa, I'm gon' be in here for a long time. I love you, and I want you to always remember that. I'll love you to the day I die."

Lisa noticed his hopeless vibe. It seemed as if he was telling her good-bye forever. "You're coming home, baby. Your lawyer is gon' file an appeal, and you're coming home."

Ray had to stop himself from becoming emotional. "That appeal is bullshit, baby. They are going to find me guilty, just like they did this time. That's even if the judge grants an appeal. Just remember, I love you, and don't let my baby girl grow up not knowing that I love her too."

Lisa looked at their daughter and then at Ray. "Tasha and I need you, Ray. You're all we got. We need you." She put her hand on the glass.

A single tear streamed down Ray's face. "*Tasha*? That's my baby girl's name? Make sure you tell her I love her. Every day, make sure that she knows that." He arose from his seat, kissed his fingers, and pressed them against the glass. He then began to walk out.

Lisa gripped the phone tightly and banged it against the glass, "No!" she screamed. "Ray, I love you! I love you!"

Ray walked back over to the glass and picked up the phone. "I love you, Lisa, but don't come here again. I don't want you or my daughter to see me in here. You deserve more. I love you." With those words he headed to the cage that would be his home for the rest of his life.

***

A few weeks later, Lisa was breast-feeding Tasha when she received a phone call. She felt the floor spinning as she tried to understand the news from the other end. When she was sure she'd heard what the voice said, she dropped the phone and fell to her knees, her baby in the other arm. "No!" she screamed as she cried. Tasha was startled by her mother's roar and began to cry too.

Ray had been stabbed to death in jail by a fellow inmate fifteen times in the chest.

Lisa sank into a deep depression and moved back home with her mother after Ray's death. She would go for weeks at a time without talking to anyone or even bathing. She often blamed herself for Ray's death, believing he wouldn't have stormed out of the house if she hadn't confronted him that night. *He would have stayed home with me,* she often thought to herself.

Lisa, looking for the same love that Ray had shown her, began to let men manipulate her into doing what they pleased. Any man who dressed nice and approached her had a chance. It became a problem when her mother grew tired of caring for Tasha while Lisa ran the streets.

Four years after Ray's death, another death was about to hit Lisa, her mother's.

When Lisa's mother died, she finally felt the burden of being a mother. Tasha had grown so attached to her grandmother, she even thought she was her mother, calling her *mama,* and Lisa by her first name.

Lisa met a man by the name of Glenn, a pimp in the neighborhood. He was in no way as successful as Ray, but Lisa was drawn to him. In some way, he reminded her of Ray.

Glenn introduced Lisa to weed. She liked the way it made her feel and began to smoke it so much, it didn't get her high anymore.

Then he introduced her to cocaine, telling her, "It makes you feel good." Lisa used to snort a little cocaine with Glenn, but that quickly grew old. Eventually she needed a new high, and Glenn provided that too. And so it was she got hooked on heroin.

ORDER FORM
URBAN BOOKS, LLC
78 E. Industry Ct
Deer Park, NY 11729

Name:(please print):_____

Address: _____

City/State: _____

Zip: _____

QTY	TITLES	PRICE
	16 On The Block	$14.95
	A Girl From Flint	$14.95
	A Pimp's Life	$14.95
	Baltimore Chronicles	$14.95
	Baltimore Chronicles 2	$14.95
	Betrayal	$14.95
	Black Diamond	$14.95
	Black Diamond 2	$14.95
	Black Friday	$14.95
	Both Sides Of The Fence	$14.95
	Both Sides Of The Fence 2	$14.95
	California Connection	$14.95

Shipping and handling-add $3.50 for 1st book, then $1.75 for each additional book.
Please send a check payable to:
    Urban Books, LLC
Please allow 4-6 weeks for delivery